Breaking

Even

Kathleen Kole

Sublime
Coyote Media

BREAKING EVEN

Copyright © 2011 by Kathleen Kole

Excerpt from *Dollars to Donuts* copyright © 2011 by Kathleen Kole

ISBN: 978-0-9868956-1-6

This book is published by Sublime Coyote Media. For more information please visit www.sublimecoyote.com.

To Peter, without whom none of this would be possible.

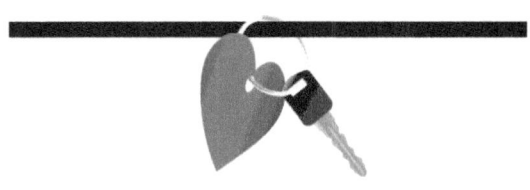

ONE

Penelope slammed her sandaled foot down onto her brakes, making her gray Volvo swerve as she narrowly missed the bumper of a maniac, car-pool Mom in an oversized, black SUV.

"Bloody Hell!" She ranted. "Did you *see* that? My God, she cut me off completely!"

Furious, Penelope rolled down her window and bellowed like a fog horn through the opening. "We're in a God-damned school zone!"

The mother behind the wheel of the SUV barely batted an eye and continued with her conversation on her cell phone.

Penelope's face was pink with suppressed irritation and she fumed silently, teeth clenched. God, *some* people! No regard for their surroundings, absolutely careless... She stopped short, when a glance into her rearview mirror revealed the wide-eyed expressions on the faces of the two young passengers in her back seat.

"Um, sorry boys," she unclenched her teeth and averted her gaze. "Do me a favor and don't repeat anything like that at school, okay?"

Kyle, eight and a half, ducked his head and snickered. He was at the age where bad words of any kind seemed not just very daring, but, also, very funny. Kevin, his younger brother by two years, nodded happily, unfazed by Penelope's outburst. Adults were always saying stuff that made no sense.

"Excellent, thank you," Penelope exhaled and crossed her fingers, hoping that she wouldn't later be facing a humble apology, to their teachers, for their new found self-expression.

"Okay," she said, purposely keeping her voice perky as she turned her attention to her task at hand, finding a parking spot. "Yes! There's one!"

Penelope rejoiced as a sedan's signal light blazed to life, declaring their imminent exit from the curbside space just ahead of her vehicle. She waited, drumming her fingers on her steering wheel, and then swiftly darted forward the moment the space was vacant.

"Okay, that's done," Penelope told the boys as she shut off the car. "Got your backpacks? We have to make a run for it before second bell, or else you'll be late and I'll have to write you excuse notes." She widened her blue-green eyes in mock horror. "How would we explain *that* to the boss?"

The boys giggled, swung the car door wide and jumped energetically to the sidewalk, leaving Penelope to rapidly shadow them as they sprinted to the school entrance.

"Have a great day," she said as she pulled on the heavy door that allowed them access into the school. "Oh, and Kyle, please remember --"

"I remember," Kyle cut her off as he hiked his Super Mario backpack across his shoulders. "If Cameron still isn't feeling well at the end of the day, Mom won't be coming to pick us up. Then, we look for you to drive us." He grinned his endearing, lopsided smile, making him look like an adorable elf. "Mom told us everything. A *lot*."

Kevin, meanwhile, took the opportunity to wrap his arms tightly around the tops of Penelope's thighs in a hug. Quite the feat, since her thighs were not the envy of any super model. Completely the opposite.

"We love you, Auntie Pen," he said, his green eyes shining as he gazed up at her.

Penelope grinned and tousled his thick, strawberry blonde hair. "You're a sweetie," she told him, before kissing him quickly on the cheek and then released him to join his brother.

The two boys waved as they were enveloped into the sea of elementary school children that flowed through the front entrance. Penelope let the heavy door swing closed and, still smiling, walked back to her car.

Penelope strolled along the footpath that encircled the school, nodding politely at the occasional parent that passed by her from the opposite direction. It was a sunny Spring morning and the buds on the shrubs around the perimeter of the school were on the verge of opening.

Come on, Spring, Penelope thought as she reached into her pocket for her cell phone. She was eager for the full onslaught of the season. She punched in a few numbers and waited, taking deep breaths of the cool, morning air. Glorious.

"Okay," she said, when Kris, her sister-in-law, picked up. "The boys are in, they're safe and they're on time." She switched her phone from her right ear to her left and reached back into her pocket for her keys. Empty.

"Thanks, so much, Pen," Kris replied, her voice tired. "I can't tell you how much I appreciate it."

"It was nothing," Penelope replied as she frowned and started checking her sweatpants for her keys.

"No, that's not true," Kris insisted, fatigue making her sound a little punch drunk. "When I called you this morning, I was at my wits end. Grayson had an early meeting and I thought I might have to send the boys to school in a cab. Can you imagine? That would have been one for the Mom gossip patrol."

Penelope laughed at the thought. "Don't mention it, really. How's Cam?"

Kris yawned loudly. "Still the same. Although, the barfing seems to have stopped, so --"

"Hell," Pen said.

"No, trust me, that's a good thing. It's *stopped* --"

"I can't believe this!"

"What?" Kris said, confused.

"I have a bad feeling ... Oh, double hell!" Penelope stopped walking and stood on the curb beside her car.

There were her keys, dangling brazenly from her ignition.

"What's going on? Are you okay?"

"Yeah, I'm fine, just --" She exhaled in frustration. "I locked my keys in the car. Actually locked them inside! Can you believe that?"

Penelope switched the phone back to her left ear and suppressed the desire to stamp her feet on the pavement like a two year old. "What am I, seventeen and a new driver?"

"Oh, I'm sorry," Kris moaned. Penelope could practically see her, pulling on her long, red hair in her remorse. "It's all my fault. If I hadn't called so last minute --"

"No," Penelope argued as she stared down at her practical, brown leather sandals. They were the first shoes that she had seen as she had rushed out the door. Thank goodness the morning wasn't any cooler, or her bare toes would have been aching. "Don't be absurd. Absolutely not. I wasn't paying attention, it had nothing to do with you."

Penelope had a sudden thought, chuckled and added, "You know, the one positive thing here is that none of my clients are around to witness this. They'd be grabbing the nearest directory and looking up 'new accountant' in a fat hurry."

Kris laughed and Penelope was glad that she'd managed to lighten the mood.

"I seriously doubt that. You're golden at your job. But, listen," Kris tried, and failed, to cover up another yawn. "Do you want me to pack up Cameron and come meet you?"

Penelope shook her head. "No. Absolutely not. You're exhausted. I'll get it handled. You stay put and take care of your son."

"You're sure --"

"I'm sure."

"Okay," Kris said. "But promise that you'll call me if you can't get things worked out and I'll find someone to help you out."

"Of course --"

"Oh, boy," Kris cut her off. "Cam's calling me. I think we may be visiting the toilet bowl again soon. Fingers crossed it's the other end this time."

Penelope shuddered and sat down on the concrete curb. Suddenly, keys locked in her car didn't seem so terrible. "You go. I'll assume I'm picking up the boys after school and see you later."

"Thanks, Pen," Kris's voice was barely audible as she hung up.

Penelope dropped her phone into her lap and rubbed her eyes. She hadn't bothered to put on mascara, or any other makeup, for that matter. Her face was naked, much like her feet. Granted, when she'd stuffed her feet into her sandals and sprinted out of the house earlier that morning, she hadn't thought that she would be sitting on the curb, wishing for socks.

"Excuse me, are you having some trouble? Do you need some help?"

Realizing that the voice was directed at her, Penelope pulled her hands from her face and turned around. Holy Dina, she thought while quickly scrambling to her feet. Apparently God did have a sense of humor. What other explanation could there have been for her being completely naked-faced, dressed in baggy, green, paint-spattered sweatpants, her unpolished toenails on display and face to face with one of the most handsome men she'd ever seen outside the pages of a magazine? Yup, comedic relief.

Penelope cleared her throat and reflexively reached up to straighten her hair. An effort that was in serious vain. Her light brown waves were secured haphazardly, courtesy of an elastic band, at the top of her head; sticking out every which-way, as though she'd suffered an electric jolt. Absolutely way beyond help.

Penelope moved on to tug self-consciously at the hem of her pale green jacket, to no avail. Forget bed-head and bohemian, she knew that she looked rumpled and frumpy.

The staggeringly tall, dark and gorgeous man watched her as she fidgeted, his hazel eyes bright and interested. "Are you okay?" He asked, and nodded encouragingly, as though she was slightly slow in her ability to understand.

"Well, umm," Penelope stammered, while inwardly cursing her sudden loss of communication skills. She must get it together! "No. I mean, yes. Yes, I'm fine and, no, I don't think I'm in trouble."

She blinked and tried not to stare. That didn't work, so, she gave up and stared. His skin, beneath the perfect, dark stubble along his jaw line, seemed to glow. Penelope wondered if it was natural, or, he went for regular facials.

The man nodded, again, which only served to encourage her need to fill in the blanks with more chatter.

"Seems I've gone and locked my keys in the car." Penelope gestured to her car's window, feeling a lot like a game show model, where the keys were in plain view. She smiled and shrugged. "Just have to get it sorted out."

He ran a hand through his thick, chocolate colored hair, his chiseled face thoughtful. "A Volvo, huh?"

The smile dropped from Penelope's face and she raised an eyebrow. "*Pardon?*"

He grinned at her and Penelope felt her knees go weak. Who cared if he wanted to judge her Volvo. His teeth were perfect, *of course*, and his dimples made her want to reach out and stroke his cheek, just to feel them.

Penelope took a small step backward when, suddenly, a thought flashed through her head. Was she being set up? She looked around suspiciously. Was that the real reason that Kris was unavailable this morning? Was she in on the gag? She glared at him and he stopped smiling.

"Okay," Penelope frowned, accusingly. "What's going on?"

He shook his head. "Sorry? I don't follow."

Penelope narrowed her eyes. "Very good. Very convincing," she said, knowingly. "However, I'm sorry to ruin your fun."

"Fun?" The man's eyebrows knotted together in a convincing expression of confusion.

"I get it," she said and folded her arms tightly across her chest. "I drive the boys to school and accidentally leave my keys in the car, which I never, ever do and, just like that, there happens to be a gorgeous, young guy - *that would be you* - available to help me out?" Penelope snorted. "Puh-leeze."

"Look," he said, raising his hands up in a 'who knows' type of shrug. "I'm not sure what you're saying. I just thought that you needed some help --"

"How old are you, anyway? You can't be more than thirty, right? Are you getting paid well for this?" Penelope looked around again, ducking and twisting to see anyone hidden out of sight in the nearby shrubbery. "How did you get my keys in the first place? Did you get a professional pick-pocket?"

He raised his eyebrows in surprise and Penelope stepped forward to peer directly at him. She had to admit, he was making a very genuine case for his confusion. Well, he was a professional, so ... Another thought floated through ... What if he wasn't acting?

"Oh, God," Penelope stopped peering and took a small step back as a sickening lump formed in her stomach. Oh, the humiliation ... "I'm wrong, aren't I?"

"Are you okay?" he questioned, his face morphing from confusion to concern. "Did you hit your head, or something? Do you need to sit back down?"

Oh good God. Penelope took a breath and hoped her voice wouldn't shake. "Listen, I'm sorry. Clearly, I got the wrong idea and I'm completely in the wrong here. You really were asking if I needed help."

He blinked a couple of times and Penelope knew that she wasn't making any sense, whatsoever, outside of her head. Jeez, some days it didn't pay to get out of bed.

"You know, maybe you're right and I should sit down." She returned to her spot on the curb and covered her face with her hands, wishing that she could disappear from sight.

The man sat down, as well; careful to leave a respectable space between them. "Okay," he said. "Admittedly, I'm feeling a bit confused."

Penelope cringed from behind her hands. Why did he stay? If the situation were reversed, she probably would have done a runner the moment the opportunity was available.

"Can we start over?"

Wow, she hadn't seen that one coming. "Yes, please," Penelope said from between her fingers. "That would be fantastic. So much less humiliating." She swallowed against her embarrassment and dropped her hands into her lap.

Okay, then, let's start over." He smiled and Penelope's stomach did a small flip. "I'm Scott. Scott Harrison." He extended a hand toward her. "And, it's just a guess, but, it looks to me like you're having a bit of trouble. Can I help?"

Penelope couldn't help but grin at his formal tone. She reached to shake his hand. "Well, thank you Scott Harrison," she bantered. "I'm Penelope Whittaker and, yes, thank you for asking. A bit of help would be great."

He laughed and released her hand, then turned his attention to her car. The keys, dangling from the ignition, seemed to be mocking her.

"That being said," Penelope shrugged. "Unless you happen to have a spare set of my keys, I'm thinking that a locksmith is going to be the way to go on this one."

Scott followed her gaze, leaned his elbows on his knees and thoughtfully rubbed his chin. "Well, we can arrange for that."

"Can I ask you something," Penelope tilted her head to one side.

"Shoot. We've been introduced."

Penelope grinned. "A few minutes ago you said, 'a *Volvo*', in a strange tone and I still cannot figure out what you meant."

"And, that explains the look you gave me when I said it." Scott chuckled. "I meant that, since your car is a Volvo, don't you actually need to be holding the keys to lock it?"

"Right," Penelope nodded as she pulled her attention from his dimples and his broad, strong shoulders ... "Well, clearly, it's not exactly a new Volvo."

Scott looked into her eyes as she spoke, giving her his full attention. Penelope was finding it extremely difficult to stay coherent when she looked back at him. She pulled her phone out of her pocket to give herself someplace else to put her eyes, besides his face.

"It's an '85, actually," She told him. "And, the safety lock is broken, so ..."

Penelope looked up from her phone to the stare at her vehicle, suddenly seeing it through fresh eyes. When had her sensible gray car become so terribly drab?

"It only just started giving me some trouble, recently." She added and, then, couldn't resist peeking upward to meet his eye. "And, I've never forgotten the keys inside, except for today, when I was rushing to drop off the kids --"

"What grade are your kids in?"

"Oh, no, I didn't mean *my* kids. No. No-no-no, God, no!" Penelope grimaced, then laughed and shook her head. "No, I don't have kids. I have *nephews*."

"Oh," Scott replied.

"But, *you* have kids, right?" Penelope said, stiffly, wishing she was wearing shoes that she could click together to make her disappear.

Scott grinned, catching her tone. "Yes, I do. A son."

"Right," she nodded, resisting the urge to pull on her hair.

"Tell me about your nephews," Scott said, kindly throwing her a lifesaver.

"My nephews," Penelope repeated and shot him a grateful look. "Well, I had to drive them here this morning, because their little brother was sick at home, and Kris, that's their Mom, didn't want to leave the house."

She caught her breath and swallowed, aware that she was starting to babble. How unsettling, she never babbled. However, in her defense, she'd never met an Adonis in the flesh, either.

"Right, okay," Scott said, when she finally went silent. "So, your sister's kids --"

"Nope. She's my sister-*in-law*, actually," Penelope corrected. "Or, to be totally accurate, *almost* sister-in-law." Her eyes darted to the substantial engagement ring that glinted on the third finger of her left hand.

"Right," Scott nodded, also glancing at her ring. "Nice rock, there."

Penelope shifted uncomfortably in her sandals and repressed the urge to hide her hand behind her back. "Thank you." She didn't know what else to add and, thankfully, Scott was still intent upon getting her story straight.

"So, let me see if I have this correct. Your *almost* sister-in-law asked you to take your *almost-nephews* to school for her and, you were so rushed, you accidentally locked your keys in your tricky Volvo and, now, you're stuck here, trying to come up with a solution?"

Penelope beamed. God, even when he was teasing, the guy was charming. And, those cheek bones, to die for. Never mind the rest of the package beneath his black track pants and red football t-shirt. Just looking at him, she could imagine his abs. Phooey. It wasn't fair, he clearly had a genetic advantage. The guy could be telling you where to go, and how to get there, and you'd *still* think he was a hunk.

"Yup," Penelope confirmed as she tucked her hands into her jacket pockets. "That's pretty much it in a nutshell. Unless, of course, you're *allergic* to nuts --"

She stopped talking when he threw his head back and laughed. It was a pleasure to watch him and she hoped she didn't look too yearning.

"You are *something*," Scott said, his tone thick with appreciation as he looked directly into her eyes.

Penelope felt her stomach flip for a second time and grinned so hard she thought her face would stay that way. She could not believe herself. She had to stop. This was so not like her, she didn't flirt.

"Sorry, by the way, for going a bit strange there," she said, attempting to regain her footing. "Clearly, I had the wrong idea about you --"

"You were charming," Scott said, his grin slow and teasing. "Not to mention, complimentary."

There goes my footing, Penelope sighed as she remembered throwing the word *gorgeous* directly at him.

"And, to answer your question," he added. "I am more than thirty. Thirty five, to be exact."

"Oh." Penelope said, and then closed her mouth. What else was she going to say to that? Something childish like, "Really? Me, too! I'm thirty five, just like you!"

"So, *Penelope*," Scott rubbed thoughtfully at the dark stubble across his chin, sparing her the opportunity to humiliate herself further. "How can I be of assistance?"

"Well," she said, gratefully following his lead. "As I said, unless you have a spare set of keys, or a lock picker under your jacket, I think I'll just have to call a locksmith and wait it out."

"As a matter of fact," Scott patted the pockets of his track pants and then shook his head. "Darn it. I thought it was here, but, sorry, I don't. Must have left it in my jacket."

"Too bad." Penelope grinned and snapped her fingers. "Maybe next time."

"Yeah," Scott shrugged. "But, listen, while you wait, do you want company?"

Penelope was taken aback by his question. She could only imagine what she looked like through his eyes. She was under no illusions, she knew what she'd looked like when she'd left the house that morning.

The paint splattered sweatpants were doing her sturdy hips no favors. Her shapeless, pale green, jacket did not highlight her blue-green eyes. As for her no-nonsense, Amish looking sandals ... Oy.

Her wardrobe, combined with her nest of hair and naked face, made Penelope wonder how it was possible that Scott had even noticed her at all. She may have been a successful accountant, but, she looked a far cry from it as that moment.

"Well," she finally managed. "If you want to stay, I can't stop you." She winced when she heard herself and quickly amended. "Okay, that came out way differently than I intended. Seriously, I don't know what's wrong with me today. I've lost control of my mouth."

Scott tilted his head slightly to one side and nodded.

Penelope wasn't sure if he was agreeing with her, or just indicating that he was listening. Either way, it made her smile as she pressed forward. "What I meant was, you sticking around and keeping me company would be great, *obviously*, but, you probably have other places you need to be. I don't want to keep you from --"

"No," Scott held his hand up and quickly assured her. "I definitely do not need to be anywhere else."

He winked at her and Penelope felt lightheaded. He had such warm, hazel colored eyes ... *Whew*.

"But," he continued. "I do think, while we wait, we could use some coffee."

"Coffee?" Penelope looked around them, in case she had missed the presence of another car, or some sort of coffee cart on wheels, parked further away. She came up with nothing. Nothing, except for her own locked Volvo and a whole lot of empty curb.

Scott nodded and flashed her another dimpled grin. "You bet. Don't go anywhere. Wait here."

Penelope grinned. "No worries."

He stood up and chuckled. "Okay, you've got me there, where else are you going to go? Right?"

Penelope shrugged and tried to soften the grin on her face that she was sure was verging on maniacal.

"Okay, maybe not that funny, but, if you don't mind waiting a minute, I'll nip into the school and then I'll be right back with refreshments." He turned toward the school and called over his shoulder. "I'll get a phone directory, too."

"I'll be right here," Penelope called back and gestured to the curb beside her car, even though he was facing the other direction. She massaged the muscles in her cheeks as she watched him walk away. Like it, or not, it was impossible not to notice that the view was stellar. Top notch.

Penelope swallowed, averted her eyes and stretched out her left hand to look at her ring, sparkling in the sunlight. You are engaged, Penelope, she chastised herself. You have no business noticing the pert, nicely shaped bums of other men.

Scott sprinted up the elementary school steps, oblivious of the power of his stellar, pert backside. He entered the school and his sneakers squeaked quietly as he walked purposefully along the deserted corridor. He had a spring in his step and was experiencing great difficulty in keeping a silly grin from spreading across his face. Despite the fact that he knew darn well he could be playing with fire - he had seen the rock on Penelope's finger - he just felt powerless to stop.

Something about this woman, something in her smile, or her eyes, or the way that she spoke ... He wasn't sure exactly, but, *something* made him want to spent more time with her. That being said, he also knew that he did not want any deep, self-examination of his motives. No nagging internal dialogue. Just coffee. Coffee and conversation. It sounded wonderful.

Scott stopped at the door to the teacher's lounge. He poked his head inside the room and nodded in satisfaction. Empty, just as he had hoped. Bless quality schools, he thought. Their staff dedication that meant that they were all where they were meant to be - in class, teaching their students.

Scott grabbed two blue, flowered mugs from a cabinet, picked up a half-full coffee pot and filled each mug. He hesitated for a moment when he realized that he hadn't asked Penelope if she took hers black, or not.

Penelope. The mere thought of her caused his stomach to flip pleasantly. Interesting. If he was honest with himself, he'd say that it had been years since he had had such a reaction to a woman. Not since Jennie...

Stop right there, Scott thought, his jaw rigid. Leave the past alone and stay in the present. He picked a telephone directory off of the counter, clamped it under his arm, tucked a few packets of sugar into his pocket and picked up the full mugs. He was all set. His pulse quickened. *Penelope*, his newly acquired acquaintance, was waiting.

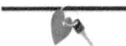

Penelope laughed so hard, that she had to set her mug on the curb for fear of covering herself in coffee. She was having such a wonderful time, she felt lightheaded. Scott had turned out to be not just breathtakingly good looking, but, fun and witty and just all around nice. Not what she had expected *at all*.

"You're making that up!" She insisted, amidst her giggles.

"I swear," Scott placed a hand on his broad chest, over his heart. "It's all true. Even the names. I didn't choose to protect the innocent."

Penelope wiped at tears of amusement as they brimmed at the edge of her eyes. Good thing she wasn't wearing mascara, after all.

"Really?" She asked, incredulous. "So, you're telling me that if I ever come across this Jason person, he will affirm your absurd tale about his trip to Vegas?"

Scott nodded, pleased as punch that he'd managed to be the source of such entertainment. Penelope was adorable when she was giggling. He figured that he would definitely need to tell Jason that he'd told his embarrassing story, but, no bother. Cross that bridge when he came to it.

"I have to say," Penelope said, her eyes sparkling. "I never thought that locking my keys in my car could have brought such --" She hesitated and bit the edge of her lip, carefully considering what words to choose.

"I know what you mean," Scott finished. "I had no idea, when I started my day, that I'd be sitting on a curb, like *this*, just being ..." He, too, was reluctant to put actual words to what they were sharing. He was just enjoying it for what it was.

They grinned at each other for a moment and then the mood was not so much broken, as thumped upon, when a large truck with the signage, "Gary's Locksmith", emblazoned on its side pulled noisily up to the curb.

Penelope jumped up and straightened her jacket, hoping that it covered the baggy backside of her sweatpants. Scott held out his hand for her mug and she reluctantly bent down to retrieve it for him. All good things had to end, she supposed.

"Hi," she said as she turned to face to the locksmith.

"That it?" The locksmith barely glanced at her as he gestured toward her car.

"Yes, that's the one."

"So," Scott began, while resisting the urge to shuffle his feet like an awkward fifteen year old. "I guess I'd better get these back to the school."

Penelope gave him her attention and nodded. "Right." She cleared her throat and quickly added, "So, um, I really appreciate you keeping me company, I really enjoyed myself."

"Me, too," he grinned.

His grin gave her the courage to finish her thought. "It was different, and unexpected, but, in a good way, you know?"

Scott understood exactly what she was trying to say. "I do know," he nodded. "Me, too."

He took a couple of steps back when the locksmith called out to Penelope.

"Okay," the guy said. "There you go. You're in."

Penelope turned and clapped her hands. "Thank you so much!"

The locksmith nodded and ambled back toward his truck.

Penelope reached into her newly opened, car door and grabbed for her purse. "Let me get my credit card for you," she rummaged in the depths of her bag and produced her wallet.

The locksmith hiked his dusty, baggy jeans - that were threatening to display too much information - up to his hips as he waited.

"Here it is!" Penelope swiftly handed over her card and then turned back toward Scott. He wasn't there. He had already begun walking back toward the school, so, she called out to him.

"Scott!"

He stopped, turned his head and smiled.

"Thanks, again. I guess I'll see you?"

Scott nodded. "Definitely. I'm sure of it."

Penelope waved as he disappeared into the school, a small grin caressing her lips. The grin transformed into a grimace when she spun around to see that the locksmith's pants were already shifting rapidly downward, back to where they had begun. Suppressing a shudder, Penelope averted her eyes and slide gratefully behind the steering wheel of her car.

Penelope pushed open Kris' back door with a flourish and strode purposefully into her kitchen. "What a beautiful day! The sun is shining, Spring is definitely in the air and I had the most amazing morning."

"Shhh!" Kris hissed, causing Penelope to stop in her tracks and clamp her lips together as she twisted her neck in the direction of the adjacent family room.

Kris was sitting on her sofa with her son, Cameron, cuddled in her arms. She was rocking him to sleep. Penelope grimaced, mouthed the word, "Sorry" and, then, twisted an imaginary key on her lips, before gently shutting the kitchen door.

Renee, Penelope's second, almost sister-in-law, was seated on a stool at the kitchen island. She gave a small wave and whispered, "Hi."

Penelope slipped off her sandals and tiptoed exaggeratedly across the tile floor to the kitchen island. "Hey," she said as she leaned up against the countertop, adjacent to Renee. "How's Cam doing?"

"Better," Renee said, softly, as she glanced at Kris. "Thank goodness kids recover from flu quickly."

Penelope nodded and fidgeted, too keyed up to pull out the neighboring stool. She gestured to a plate of chocolate chip cookies, on the island top. "Are those up for grabs?"

"Uh-huh," Renee said, softly, and then raised an eyebrow. "Although, you seem to be full of beans. Sure you want to add sugar and chocolate to that equation?"

Penelope pulled off her jacket, draped it across the back of a chair and chose a cookie from the pile. "I know, you're probably right, but, I've only had coffee today. I should have something with some fiber in it to help my buzz."

Kris stood up and, with well-practiced precision, placed Cameron onto the sofa and covered him with a soft blanket. The three year old boy's eyes were closed, his breathing calm and rhythmic. She sighed. There was a light at the end of the tunnel.

"Whew, okay," she walked into the kitchen and picked up a hairband from the granite countertop. "Sorry about that Pen, but, I just needed to get him to sleep. We can talk freely now. Once he's out, it would take the equivalent of a bomb to wake him. Thank God for small blessings."

"He's doing better?" Penelope asked as she finished her cookie and reached for another.

Kris slicked her long, red hair into a ponytail with her hairband and retrieved a bag of coffee from her cupboard. "Thank goodness, yes." She turned to face Penelope. "So, you're here, does that mean you got the situation with your car sorted out?"

"What happened?" Renee asked.

"She dropped off the boys at the school, for me, and then her car keys got locked inside her vehicle."

Penelope leaned forward, willing and eager to share. "That was only the tip of the iceberg! After that, I had the most unexpected and bizarre morning!"

"Clearly," Kris grinned. "Did the school threaten to have you towed?"

Penelope laughed and brushed cookie crumbs from her fingers onto a used napkin on the island. "No, but, that is where it happened."

"Where what happened?" Kris said. "More car trouble?"

"No," Penelope said as she started to pace around the kitchen.

Renee, short, curvy and resembling a raven haired pixie, looked up from a sketch pad in front of her and raised an eyebrow.

"I met a guy," Penelope raved, her eyes wide with excitement. "This amazing, hubba-hubba, gorgeous single dad. At the school. Right after I dropped off the kids and locked my keys in the car."

Renee dropped her pencil on her sketch pad, rested her chin in her hand and narrowed her eyes. She didn't like Penelope's vibe. Not one bit.

"Was this guy, this 'Single Dad', there when you called me?" Kris asked as she measured coffee and water into her coffee maker.

"No." Penelope shook her head. "It wasn't until after we hung up, and I was sitting on the curb, like a truant school child, that he showed up."

Kris chuckled at Penelope's imagery.

Renee frowned. She found it unsettling that Penelope was acting like a giddy, school girl. A giddy, *single* school girl. Her behavior was very out of character, not to mention, just downright weird.

"Okay," Kris said as she measured coffee and water into her coffee maker. "So, you met this hunky Single Dad, and then what happened?"

"That's the thing," Penelope gushed. "I wasn't that I met him. He *met me*."

"Oh," Kris nodded. "Okay, so, he hit on you."

"No!" Penelope stopped pacing and took a breath. The way Kris said it made it sound ... cheap.

"No?"

Penelope tried, again. "He offered to help me out with my car --"

"How?"

Penelope paused to look at Renee. "Pardon?"

"How," Renee reiterated. "Did this guy --"

"Single Dad," Kris clarified, her voice teasing and laced with amusement at the title.

Penelope reached out and slapped her playfully on the shoulder.

Renee raised an eyebrow and huffed. "Fine, how did Single Dad even know that you needed help?"

"Oh, okay," Penelope said. "Well, I guess he saw me sitting there and deduced that I was in need of assistance --"

"Does this guy have a name that we can use, by chance?" Renee asked, as she made the effort to smooth the frown from her brow.

"Of course!" Penelope gushed, happy that they were getting back on track. "His name is Scott."

"I like Single Dad, better," Kris offered.

Penelope smirked, but, refused to take the bait. "Anyway, after he knew I needed help, we started chatting and --"

"Still sounds a lot like he was hitting on you," Kris reiterated.

"It wasn't like that," Penelope insisted. "Even when there was nothing that he could do and he could have left, he chose to stay with me while I waited for the locksmith. He even got us coffee and it was just ..."

"Got you coffee?" Renee said. "From where?"

"Uh-huh," Penelope said, a goofy grin plastered on her face. "From inside the school."

Renee bit her tongue. She wanted to declare to Penelope that this guy, Single Dad, sounded pretty darned slick and skilled at being charming. But, she didn't. She kept her thoughts to herself. Instead, she asked a very pointed question.

"Did he happen to notice that you're wearing a very large and gorgeous engagement ring?"

Penelope placed her hands on her hips and exhaled sharply. "Yes, Renee, he saw my ring." She held up her hand and her diamond sparkled in the light. "It's pretty hard to miss."

"So, after the locksmith," Kris said, trying to soothe the sudden tension. "Then, what happened?"

"It was strange and, yet, not," Penelope told her. "Does that make sense?"

"No," Renee said.

Penelope ignored her. She was getting a negative vibe from Renee and, quite frankly, didn't want to address it. "Well, it was strange in that, we talked about stuff, any old stuff, like we'd known each other for years. Even though, clearly, we don't."

Kris' face grew thoughtful and she nodded. "I remember doing that, just talking and talking about anything at all, when I first met Grayson."

Penelope absentmindedly ran her index finger back and forth across her bottom lip. "And, when I think of how I *look*," she gestured to her sloppy clothes and wayward hair. "God, the mere fact that he stopped at all had to be some sort of miracle."

Renee sat up in her chair. The comparison of Kris and her husband, to Penelope and some guy *who was not her fiancé*, wasn't lost on her for a moment. The whole thing, in her opinion, had turned a corner and she had to try to give some relativity back to the conversation. She wracked her brain, trying to come up with something. Something, that is, other than, 'What the hell are you talking about?'

"Did you give the cups back to the school?" Kris asked.

"Scott did, I think," Penelope replied as she pulled the elastic from her hair, releasing it from its confines to burst messily around her face. She took another cookie from the plate. "To be honest with you, by that time I was so in over my head, he could have made them disappear into thin air and I wouldn't have blinked."

Kris grinned at Penelope and retrieved three cups from her cupboard. "Yeah, I got that, loud and clear."

Renee turned to Kris. She needed some answers. "Have you heard about this guy, Single Dad? Is he on the grid, or just some slick dude --"

"He's not!" Penelope blurted, then winced as she glanced across to Cameron's sleeping form on the family room couch. He didn't move and she felt a wave of relief that she hadn't woken him.

Kris shrugged. "I don't think so. Doesn't ring a bell."

"He said that he's new to the area," Penelope informed Renee. "His wife passed away years ago, about a year after their son was born."

Renee grimaced and Penelope nodded, the untamed waves of her hair bouncing around her face. "Oh, yeah, believe me, I *know*. Even worse, I found that out *after* I had shuddered dramatically, shoved my foot in my mouth and said I didn't have kids."

Penelope closed her eyes and pressed her fingertips against them in an attempt to shut out the memory of her embarrassment. "And, hang onto your seats, because the embarrassment doesn't stop there."

Renee hopped off her stool to stretch. "There's more?"

Penelope pulled her hands from her face and nodded. "When he first showed up, before we actually starting talking and all of that, I accused him of trying to prank me."

"What?" Kris had started pouring coffee and stopped, the pot poised above her cup. She looked at Penelope, incredulous. "Prank you? What does that even mean?"

"I couldn't wrap my head around the way that everything had unfolded." Penelope twisted a piece of hair round and round her finger. It was so humiliating.

"It just suddenly seemed too perfectly orchestrated. There I was, stranded, and mister over-the-top gorgeous turns up, exactly at the right moment."

"So, you --" Kris prompted.

"So, *I*," Penelope nodded. "Got all righteous and accused him of trying to set me up. To prank me."

Kris couldn't help herself and snickered. "Sorry, I know you don't think it's funny, but, oh my God, Pen!"

"I know," Penelope rolled her eyes. "I can't believe I did it either. It was just that he arrived too conveniently, you know?"

"I can just imagine it," Kris giggled. "You ... his face when you accused him ... I can't stand it!"

Penelope rolled her eyes. "Thank God he was gracious and ignored my rambling, or, I don't know what I would have done. As it was, I wanted the ground to open up and swallow me, that's for sure. But, as I said, he was gracious and asked if we could start over ..." She beamed and her eyes lit up with pleasure. "Then, the rest of the morning went pretty much how I told you."

Renee went to the fridge for coffee cream and watched Penelope with a close eye. Something else was going on. She just knew it. She had known Penelope for a lot of years and she had never seen her so skittish. Especially over a man.

Kris took a deep breath and shook her head. "God, Pen, warn a girl before you do that. I'm too tired for that kind of amusement."

Penelope laughed and Renee decided that subtle attempts to pull things back to reality weren't working. It was time to be blunt.

"Okay," Renee said, as she placed the cream carton on the kitchen island. "So, we know that he's a widower and he has a child. Sounds like a full plate."

Penelope opened her mouth to respond, but, Renee swiftly cut her off. "Don't envy the woman who gets into *that*. A lot of baggage and history there."

"That's true," Kris agreed, passing a cup to each of them. "It couldn't be easy to follow a dead wife."

"His son is five," Penelope said as she reached for the cream. "So, I'd hazard to guess that, since it's been four years since she passed away, he's through the mourning period."

Renee ran her fingers through her short, black hair. "Has he actually been dating since she passed away? Does he have a girlfriend? Did he talk about that? Some men hold on a lot longer than others."

Penelope shook her head as she poured cream into her coffee. "I'm not sure. We didn't get that personal, just the surface facts. But, that being said, I did have this strange thing happen. I had a sort of running commentary going through my head the entire time."

"Ah," Kris said as she picked up her coffee cup and sat down gracefully on a chair adjacent to Renee. Regardless of the fact that she'd given birth to three children, the woman had retained the slim build of a model. Had she not been Penelope's best friend, she might have had to hate her.

"Do you know what I mean by that?" Penelope asked as she fished a spoon from a drawer. "Does that make any sense to you? Have you ever had that?"

"No," Renee said, bluntly as she poured cream into her own cup.

"I've had the commentary thing," Kris said. "It's like you're constantly assessing, to figure out if what you are saying is really you, or, some sort of alternate universe you."

"Exactly!" Penelope enthused.

Kris took a sip from her cup and glanced at the drawing on Renee's paper. "God, you're ridiculous. You make it look so easy! Pen, look at this cake, it's fantastic. I know you love the baking, Ren, but, you should have a showing of your sketches, too. They're art."

Penelope began to pace, again, in circles around the island. "You explained it perfect, Kris. That's exactly what it was like. An alternate universe Me. And, mine kept on saying things like, 'What are you doing, *Penelope*? This isn't like you. What about Ben?'" She stopped and shook her head. "It was exhausting."

"That's a valid question, you know. What about Ben?" Renee jumped at her chance.

"What? What's there to be about?" Penelope stopped pacing and looked at her, confused. "It wasn't like I ran off with the man --"

"But, you had the *thought*." Kris looked at her, with the kind of knowing that can only come from being a friend to someone for as many years as they had been friends, and Penelope felt a shiver run up her spine.

Apparently, she really was as transparent as plastic wrap.

Renee was so happy that Kris had picked up the issue that she had been trying, and failing, to address, she could have kissed her.

"And," Kris added. "Even if it was just for a moment that you had the thought, that's definitely something to consider, don't you think? After all you're engaged to be *married*. How would you feel if Ben felt like that about another woman?"

Penelope recoiled at the suggestion. It had not ever occurred to her. She put down her coffee cup and glanced at a flower shaped clock on the kitchen wall. "God, look at the time --"

"Avoiding." Renee felt it was safe to say it, since Kris would back her up. She picked up her coffee cup and noted that Penelope looked very uncomfortable with the turn of the conversation. "Not a good sign, Penelope."

"Am not." Penelope shot back and pulled her elastic off her wrist, to twist around her unstinted hair. "I'm was just thinking, I have a couple of things I need to do, not to mention shower, before I go and get Kyle and Kevin from school."

"Oh, that's okay, you don't have to bother." Renee looked Penelope directly in the eye and watched for her reaction. "I can call Paul and ask him to pick up the boys for Kris. He'll be there, anyway, getting our girls, so it works out perfectly."

"Are you sure that's such a good idea?" Penelope asked and then turned her attention to putting on her jacket, so that she could ignore both of their smug expressions. "That's three different classrooms and four kids. I think it might just be easier if I go."

Kris rolled her eyes and snickered. "Yeah, *easier.*"

Pen cut her eyes at Kris and she slapped her hand across her mouth to keep her laughter contained. She didn't want to wake her sleeping son.

Against her better judgment, she was still annoyed at their leading questions, Penelope couldn't help herself and grinned. "Oh, both of you, shut up."

"So," Renee commented, once Penelope had left. "What did you make of all that?"

Kris had moved Cameron to his bedroom and was attempting to clear away the human detritus left behind by her family earlier that morning. She needed to get things in order before they all returned home, again, and added more.

"What are we talking about?" Kris asked as she swept crumbs from the table and then threw down a wet cloth to scrub vigorously at the remaining sticky surface.

"Penelope. She seemed really thrown off kilter by that guy," Renee said, matter-of-factly.

Kris paused to rinse out her cloth at the sink and pondered what Renee had said. "You mean, Single Dad?"

Renee nodded.

"Yeah, I guess so. No question, she was giddy. But, all teasing aside, I don't think --"

"Exactly," Renee cut her off. "She *was* giddy. Unnaturally so. I don't think I've ever seen her like that, it was so unlike her." Renee looked thoughtful. "You've known her even longer than I have, am I possibly making more of it, than it is?"

"I'm not sure," Kris replied. "What it is that you think you're possibly making more of?"

Renee erased a couple of lines on her sketch pad as she pondered the question. Kris continued to clean as she waited.

"I guess," Renee said. "I'm just thinking that, since I've never seen her that way, not even with Ben, it could mean trouble. Again, maybe I'm seeing something that wasn't there."

Kris paused and cocked her head. "Huh ... You know, now that you mention it, I've never seen her like that over Ben, either."

"Although," Renee chewed on the end of her pencil. "That being said, I might be acting short sighted and not be considering the other side of it."

Kris raised an eyebrow, intrigued. "And, that would be?"

"If the situation presented itself, the way it did with Penelope and Single Dad, would I be just like her and react, too? Would you?"

"Do you mean actually feel something real for the guy?"

Renee's face creased with concern. "Oh-my-God! Did you say real feelings? Because, that's what I was worried about, I just didn't want to say it out loud."

Kris dropped her cloth and held out her hand. "Wait a minute --"

"So, it wasn't just me, you got that vibe, too?" Renee asked, wide eyed. "Do you think that's what happened to Pen? She actually *felt* something for the guy? Not just girly, flirty stuff, but, *real* stuff?"

"Whoa! Back up, I'm confused," Kris tried to back pedal their conversation. "What the hell are we talking about?"

Renee nodded her head, slowly, as everything clicked into place. "You're right, you know."

"Right? How am I right? About what?"

"Now that we're saying it out loud, there was no questioning the way Pen was acting, or, what she was saying. She did actually *feel* something. God, I didn't want to actually admit it --"

"No," Kris protested, weakly. "No, I didn't say that. And, I don't think that. I'm tired. I've been up with Cameron. I just misunderstood what you said."

"And," Renee continued as though Kris hadn't spoken. "If that's what happened, it could mean something bad for her relationship with Ben. They've been engaged for *forever*, its been what now? Three years? And, they haven't even set a date. What if Single Dad is a catalyst --"

"Stop," Kris waved her hands back and forth. "Seriously, we have to stop. We're reading way more into this than necessary." She picked up her cloth and started wiping vigorously, again, at the just cleaned countertops. "All Penelope did was share that she'd met a cute Dad--"

"Mister, *over-the-top-gorgeous*, Single Dad."

"And," Kris' voice was firm as she ignored Renee and continued to scrub. "We're making a big deal out of it, when it's nothing. She admitted that she flirted a bit, big deal, and here we are, imagining her running off with the guy! Come on, this is Penelope we're talking about, for goodness sake. Please."

Renee sighed and nodded. "Okay, fine. You're probably right. We're reading more into this than necessary. It was just silly flirting, probably nothing."

"*Definitely* nothing," Kris insisted as she moved from scrubbing, to gathering up dirty plates and bowls left behind from breakfast earlier that morning. While Grayson was a fabulous husband and always stepped up to the plate when Kris needed him, he had a definite blind spot for cleaning up behind the kids.

"Right," Renee said. It was time to change the subject. "So, enough about that. How about you?"

Kris pulled open the door to her dishwasher and looked questioningly at Renee. "What do you mean?"

Renee raised an eyebrow and hopped down from her stool. She picked up some stray cups and glasses to add to Kris' pile and waited.

Kris took the dishes and added them to the dishwasher. "I'm fine, other than going a little nutty. It's ridiculous, really, since I clearly have enough to do around here."

"It's not ridiculous," Renee stated. "It's normal."

Kris shrugged. "I guess the issue I'm having is that my mind is restless. I'm physically busy, but, I need something besides the daily drudgery. I can do this on auto-pilot."

"Do you know how many stay-at-home Moms I've heard say the same thing?"

"You don't say it."

"Yes, but, I'm not a good example. I have *Divine Designs* and that gives me my creative, non-Mom, outlet."

"That's what I'm saying," Kris said as she added detergent to the dishwasher. "I've become a cliché. Maybe I should start a sewing circle, not that I can sew worth a damn. Or, a scrap-booking club, even though the very idea makes my skin crawl --"

Renee watched Kris with amused eyes. The woman had energy to burn. "Charity work! A book club!" She decided to throw more ideas into the mix.

Kris' face lit up. "A book club! Actually, that's not a bad idea. I love to read and I'm sure that there are some Moms at the school who do, too."

Renee felt regret that she'd blurted out her idea. It was a good one, but, still, as a long term thing, she didn't think it held a hope of dispelling Kris' need for something of her own.

"Would you join?"

Renee swallowed uncomfortably. "Well, truthfully, I don't know if I'd have the time." She gestured weakly toward her sketch pad and gave an apologetic smile.

Kris waved her hand dismissively. "Of course you wouldn't! God, I'm sorry, I shouldn't have even asked. But, then, I didn't want you to think I was going to steal your idea and not even include you --"

Renee shook her head. "No worries, steal away. But, you have to promise me something."

Kris cocked her head and waited.

"No gorgeous men at your book club to cause an uprising of silly, giggly Moms."

Kris grinned. "Deal."

Renee gathered up her sketch pad and pencils. "I should really get going," she said and tucked her materials into her large, soft leather messenger bag.

"Thanks for listening."

"No trouble." Renee reached out and squeezed Kris's hand affectionately. "You'll get it all in order, you'll see. These things have a way of working themselves out. I think that there's an opportunity right around the corner for you that will fit perfectly into your life."

Kris nodded and Renee left it at that. She had some very real ideas as to how Kris could begin her journey back into the working work. However, to use Winston Churchill's favorite quote, *timing is everything.*

Penelope leaned against her car and hoped she wasn't getting dirt on her black trousers. She also hoped that she looked nonchalant, as opposed to uncomfortable and contrived. After she'd left Kris' kitchen, she had motored home to shower and change and find something better to wear than her sweatpants and wrinkled jacket. Not that she was changing for anyone in particular. No, she told herself, she would be facing a lot of parents and she had cleaned up for herself.

The school bell rang and Penelope breathed deeply, attempting to steady her nerves. Stay calm, she told herself as children began to rapidly litter the pavement around her. No need to look like a tourist in a crowd, craning your neck in an embarrassing manner as you try to spot the hottie amongst the parental fray.

As fate would have it, instead of finding the hottie, Penelope spotted Kyle and Kevin. The boys waved and came running over, breathless and excited to see her.

"Auntie Pen," Kyle's sky blue eyes widened as he looked at her smart, crisp trousers and clingy, dark purple blouse. "You look so pretty!"

"And, tall," Kevin added as he checked out the two inch heels of her black, suede boots.

Pen giggled, amused by her nephews enthusiasm. "Don't sound so surprised, guys. I do get out of my sweatpants from time to time, you know."

"Uh-huh," Kyle nodded, in a perfect imitation of a knowing adult. "But, you look so," he paused to think of the word, his eight year old face serious.

"Girlie!" Kevin supplied, pleased with himself.

Kyle nodded decisively at his younger brother. "Yeah, that's it, *girlie.*"

Pen smoothed her blouse and ran a hand lightly through her freshly washed and tamed hair. "Well, I think I'll just say thanks and we'll leave it at that, okay?"

She spun on her heel and reached to open the car door, just as a deep voice invaded her thoughts for a second time that day. "Good to see. Doors open and not a locksmith in sight."

A shiver ran up Penelope's spine and did not go unnoticed by Kyle. "Are you cold, Auntie Pen? Did you forget your jacket?"

"No, I'm fine." Penelope glanced over her shoulder at Scott and felt her stomach lurch. Dressed in faded, slim cut jeans, an open collared dress shirt and well worn, brown leather jacket, he was as gorgeous as she had remembered. "Get in the car, boys. I'll be right there."

The two boys scuttled into her backseat and dragged their backpacks behind them. Penelope closed the door, swallowed her nerves and turned to face Scott.

"Nope, no need for assistance this time," she bantered, a Cheshire grin spreading across her face when his eyes revealed surprise and appreciation at how she looked. He swept his eyes down and up her body, his gaze lingering momentarily at the ample cleavage she had on display, and Penelope knew that her efforts had been worth every minute spent.

She held open her palm to reveal her car keys. "I think I've learned my lesson."

Scott chuckled, his laughter low and intimate, and Pen suppressed another shiver. "Glad to know I was around for the lesson," he teased. "If you have any more you want to share, just let me know."

Penelope was at a loss as to how to respond. It had been years since she'd flirted to this extent. So many, she had lost count. Besides, she suddenly thought, as everything came into focus, what was she doing trying to flirt, anyway? She was *engaged*, for goodness sake!

"Hey, there he is," Scott waved at someone behind her, giving Penelope a chance to catch her breath. "How was the day, buddy?"

Penelope watched as Scott placed an affectionate hand on a young boy's shoulder. He had to be his son. There was no mistaking it, the child was the spitting image of his father with his dark hair and sparkling, hazel eyes. He was beautiful.

"This is my son," Scott said, smiling proudly.

Bingo, Penelope thought. She'd called it. She nodded and smiled at the boy. "Hi, nice to meet you. I'm --"

"Pen?"

Penelope jumped at the unexpected sound of her name and snapped her head to her right. She had been in a near trancelike state, with Scott and his son, and she blinked a couple of times when she saw Paul, Renee's husband, walking purposefully toward her.

"What are you doing here?" Paul asked her, looking extremely lawyerly and intimidating in his well-cut, dark suit. He frowned slightly and gave Scott the once-over.

Penelope had been about to ask him the same question. "Picking up the boys for Kris!" She gestured wildly at her car as though offering proof. Kyle and

Kevin, waiting patiently in the backseat, beamed and waved to their Uncle.

Paul nodded, flicked his eyes in the boy's direction, then returned his steady, unflinching gaze to Scott. Oh, boy. Penelope figured she'd better act fast.

"Anyway, Paul," she said and hoped her voice didn't betray her nerves. "This is Scott. Scott," she gestured to Paul. "This is Paul, my brother-in-law."

"Don't you mean, *almost* brother-in-law?" Scott teased, raising a knowing eyebrow.

Oh, shit, Penelope thought, as Paul's face took on a look of thunder. Time for damage control, and quickly, before Paul attempted to *do* damage to Scott.

"So, anyway," she breezed by Scott's comment and turned to Paul. "I'm here for the boys, since Kris is at home with Cam."

"I could have picked them up with the girls," Paul stated. He was standing with his feet spaced widely apart, his arms folded across his chest, like a well-dressed gladiator. "No need for you to take off work to do it."

"Oh, I know, Renee mentioned it earlier this morning," Penelope assured him, patting his arm. "But, it just so happened that my clients today were easy to juggle, so, here I am."

"Not to mention," Scott offered, his tone warm and familiar. "When you locked yourself out of your car, you really had no choice but to take off work, right?"

Paul narrowed his eyes at Scott and then turned to Penelope, his voice practically accusatory. "What's that about? Did something happen that you needed help with today?"

Penelope felt herself beginning to sweat beneath her silky blouse. Things were happening too quickly for her to control. "No, no, it was nothing --"

"We got it handled," Scott squared his shoulder and nodded confidently at Paul.

Jeez, Penelope winced when Paul's nostrils flared. Was he trying to make him angry?

"So, Sport," Scott turned to his son, effectively shutting down the conversation. "Time for us to head home."

Yes, please, Penelope thought. *Leave*.

Scott smiled and briefly touched Penelope's arm. "Good to see you again, so soon, Penelope."

Before she could form a reply, he stole another quick glance at her cleavage and, then, quickly pulled his eyes away to meet Paul's stare. "Good to meet you."

"Auntie Pen?" Kevin rolled down the car window and called from Penelope's backseat. "We're hungry, can we go for burgers before we go home?"

Bless you, Penelope thought, and took the opportunity Kevin offered, to turn away from the uncomfortable tableau in front of her.

"Yes, I think so," she replied. "I'll just have to call your Mom first to make sure it's okay."

She pulled her cell phone from her pocket and braced herself as she turned back toward Scott and Paul. Who knew what she would find.

"Not *just* the chauffeur today, apparently --" she started, then tapered off when she realized she was talking to nothing but air.

They were gone. Penelope quickly scanned the people who remained on the sidewalk, but, still, neither man was anywhere to be seen. That was fast.

"Well, what'd she say?" Kyle prompted from the back seat.

"Just getting to it," Penelope said and pressed the automatic dial on her phone. She thought of the look on Paul's face and felt a flutter of nervousness in her belly. What would he say to Renee? Would he think that there was anything *to* say? He'd been so stoic, there was no question in her mind that he had been bothered, in a major way, by her being with Scott. Not that she had actually *been* with Scott, of course, circumstances had just come together to make it appear that way.

Penelope sighed and held the phone to her ear, grateful to that she could turn her thoughts toward burgers and milkshakes.

Ben Miller tapped his steering wheel, keeping time with the beat of the song that flooded the interior of his Audi A4. He'd had one hell of a hectic day - productive, but, hectic. Whomever might have thought that a career as a CPA was dull, hadn't spent a day in his corporate shoes.

Ben let the lyrics from U2's "One" wash over him as he pressed the automatic dial on his cell phone. He knew he should probably be listening to Top 40 music to stay current, but, the music from his youth made him happy. He ran a hand across his short, surfer-blonde hair, hummed along and waited for the sound of Penelope's voice. He got her voicemail.

"Hey, Honey," he said, stifling a sigh, as he spoke into the headset attached to his ear. He did not like voice mail. "Just in traffic, it's moving steadily, and I thought I'd give you a quick call to let you know I'll be home soon." He stopped at a red light and loosened his tie. "Looking forward to seeing you, love you."

Ben hung up and glanced at the huge bouquet of flowers on the adjacent passenger seat. They were a mixture of blooms, in radiant colors of yellow, orange and red; not unlike the last rays of the sunset outside his windows. He was trying to add an element of surprise to his fiancée's day, throwing a bit of the unexpected into their routine. Something had to start the ball rolling to shake up their pattern.

He and Penelope had been missing each other a lot more than usual, their work schedules allowing them only snippets of time each day to connect and catch up. Ben was concerned that the habit was becoming a new sort of normal and wanted to stop it in its tracks.

Regardless of the fact that they were both career oriented people, he didn't want to become the type of couple who put their relationship second. He had watched it happen to friends and the next step was always the same - splitting up.

Not an option, Ben thought as the light turned green and he accelerated forward toward home. He'd been waiting patiently for a long time, years, for Penelope to make a decision about when they would have their wedding. The very idea that their work lives might interfere and be the cause of that not coming to pass ... He exhaled sharply. Absolutely not an option.

Kris' husband, Grayson, leaned casually against his open front door. He was still in his work clothes - an expensive, and expertly tailored, charcoal grey suit; paired with a sage green, equally expensive and expertly tailored, dress shirt. His clothes, in combination with his short, dark blonde hair and the beginning of a five o'clock shadow across his sharp jaw, gave the man the looks of a model.

"Thanks again, Pen," he said as Kyle and Kevin trudged past them into the house, lugging their backpacks. "Say thank you to Auntie Penelope, guys."

Penelope shook her head. "It's fine. They already did. See you soon, boys," she called. "Thanks for the company."

Kyle and Kevin dropped their school things onto the hardwood floor and waved as they charged upstairs, jockeying for first place to the top. Grayson shook his head at their laziness, but, his blue eyes sparkled and his face held an affectionate grin, revealing his true feelings. "Guess they think the help will get their stuff."

"And, she probably will," Penelope smiled and leaned her shoulder against the door frame. "So, how's Cam doing since this morning?"

"He's over the worst of it. He's a strong little guy." Grayson rubbed the stubble on his chin and nodded confidently. "Wouldn't be surprised if he's up and running around as usual in the next couple of days."

Penelope covered her mouth with her hand and yawned. It had been a long day. "Good. I'm glad. Make sure Kris gets some rest, too. Even if you have to super glue her to her chair."

"I'll tell her you said so." He chuckled when she yawned a second time. "Looks like you could use some rest, too."

Penelope grinned and tried to shake off her tiredness. "Whew! I know. Those two boys don't stop. The questions, the chatter about school, they took it out of me."

Grayson nodded appreciatively. "Tell me about it. I don't know if they're keeping us young, or driving us more swiftly into old age." He leaned in and gave her a quick hug. 'You look great, by the way. New client today?"

Penelope smiled. That was so Grayson. He was the type of man who always noticed the small things, like a woman's hair or clothing, and was willing to offer a compliment. Never mind his leading man looks, it was that trait, that charm, which seriously contributed to his success in business.

"Thanks," she said. "But, no, just a normal day. I felt like airing out something besides my usual conservative accountant attire, so ..."

Grayson smiled. "It suits you. I'm sure that brother of mine thinks so, too."

At the mention of Ben's name, Penelope felt a wave of guilt wash over her. If only Paul hadn't been at the school ... A moment of cold dread barreled in swiftly behind her guilt and rolled across her skin as she remembered the look on Paul's face when he had registered Scott's presence. Penelope was certain that had it been Grayson meeting Scott, he would have been just as protective and unwelcoming as his brother.

Grayson yawned and then laughed. "Apparently, it's catching."

"I think that's my cue and I should get going," Penelope said, shoving her unsettling thoughts aside as she backtracked down the front steps.

"Tell Ben I'll call him soon, okay?"

"Sure," Penelope said as she almost ran down the front path to her car. Any more mention of Ben and she was worried she'd start confessing to a crime she hadn't committed.

"Drive safe," Grayson called out, just before she closed her car door. Penelope pretended she hadn't heard and sped away without a backward glance.

Renee watched Paul from the corner of her eye as she served their seven year old, twin daughters their dinner. He looked agitated. "Girls, there's bread on the counter, as well, if you want it."

The two little girls jumped up from their seats at the table, their matching, brunette ponytails swishing madly, and made a dash for the bread. "Hey!" Paul said. "Slow down, it's not a race."

Zoe and Alexa giggled as they shuffled their purple slipper clad feet across the tile floor to the kitchen island. Renee couldn't help but giggle along with them, they were such goofballs.

"So," she ventured. "How was your day?"

"Oh, it was fine. Busy, but, fine." Paul twisted spaghetti noodles around his fork and Renee waited. There was more.

"I saw Penelope at the school this afternoon." He forked his noodles into his mouth and went silent as he chewed.

Renee nodded, patient. She'd been married to the man for almost nine years, she knew that that wasn't all he was going to offer.

Alexa and Zoe climbed back into their respective seats at the table, bread in hand, and Renee got up to retrieve the butter. "Oh, right," she said, casually, over her shoulder. "She was in charge of Kyle and Kevin today, for Kris. Cameron was sick."

Paul swallowed and nodded. "Yeah, that's what she said when I spoke to her and her *friend*."

Oh, dear. Renee had a sinking feeling. The way that Paul had said, 'her *friend*', did not sound good. Renee had a strong hunch that the *friend* in question was dreaded Single Dad. Her hunches were rarely wrong.

"*Friend*, right," Paul muttered, under his breath, as he twisted more pasta on his fork.

Renee kept her voice light and placed the butter dish on the table. "A colleague?"

Paul glanced at his daughters to see if they were listening. They weren't. They had pulled the lid off of the dish Renee had set in front of them and were focused upon slathering butter on every square inch of their bread slices.

"Don't think so. She definitely referred to the guy as a friend." Paul scowled, pulled his fork out of his pasta and pointed it at Renee. "But, between you and me, he was not looking at her in a friendly manner."

Renee sat down, smoothed her napkin onto her lap and noted that their daughters had lost interest in their bread, in favor of she and Paul's conversation. "Was he not being nice to Auntie Penelope? Because, sometimes, at school, some of the boys don't act very friendly."

Alexa stuffed some of her bread into her mouth, coating her lips in butter, and attempted to speak around it. "Like Jordan," she mumbled.

Zoe nodded and nibbled at her bread slice. "And, his brother, Jason. He's a brat."

"Alexa, please! Chew and swallow." Renee grimaced as she watched her daughter, doing a fine imitation of a hamster. They spent so much time with their boy cousins that, unfortunately, a lot of their uncivilized habits rubbed off on the girls.

Paul took a sip of his wine and shook his head. "No, he wasn't being mean or anything, to Auntie Penelope. Just more *familiar*, than friendly. If you know what I mean."

The two girls frowned in confusion and Paul smiled. They looked like matching, dark haired bookends.

"Anyway, it was probably nothing," he said, putting an end to the topic. "Just Daddy being silly. How were the days of my best girls?"

Renee slowly released her breath as their daughters began to vie for Paul's attention. She knew that he wasn't done. He'd want more information. However, for the moment, in the interest of little pitchers having big ears, he was putting it aside. Thank goodness.

That would give her some time to reform the information that Penelope had doled out, to she and Kris, earlier that morning. Renee figured that she could tweak it and turn it into an amusing anecdote and, hopefully, that would be the last time anyone in her family made reference to Single Dad.

"Hello?" Ben called out as he pushed open the door that separated the garage from the house. "Pen? You home?" He shucked off his leather jacket and hung it on a hook in the front hallway.

"In here," Penelope answered, her voice tired and flat. The day had finally caught up with her. She was chopping celery for a stir fry and listening with one ear to the news on the TV in the family room.

Ben bounded into the kitchen. "Man, what a day! It was hectic, but, worth it. You remember that client I was telling you about, John Stiles? Well, he was over the moon with the way I managed to work with his numbers and it looks like we'll be getting all of his firm's business, from now on."

"Great," Penelope said, without looking up from the celery.

Ben grinned and pulled off his loosened tie. "These, by the way, are for you!" He pulled the bouquet of lavish flowers from behind his back with a flourish.

Penelope stopped chopping and stared, completely surprised. "What are those for?"

"Because I love you and want you to remember that I do."

Penelope wiped her hands on a dish towel hanging on the oven door and gave Ben a small smile. "Well, they're gorgeous. Thank you."

"My pleasure."

She reached out and he placed them into her hand. "I'll grab a vase from the cupboard."

"You okay?" Ben opened the fridge, reached in and pulled out a beer.

"Yes, I'm fine. Why?"

Ben twisted the top off his beer and shrugged. "I don't know, you seem distracted, or something. Maybe tired? You look tired."

Penelope's spirits immediately took a nosedive. Granted, her hair was pulled messily into a clip, she was no longer wearing her pretty clothes and had changed into her baggy, pink fleece pants and an oversized t-shirt, but, still, *tired?*

She whirled around, her flowers still clutched in her hand. "Oh, *nice*, Ben!"

Ben took a step back, surprised. "What?"

"You look *tired?* Really?"

Ben held up a hand. "Oh, come on, I didn't say it like *that* --"

"You don't think so? Because, it sure sounded like it to me." Penelope glared at him, then yanked a vase out of a cabinet and slammed it into the sink.

Ben flinched. "Pen, come on, I didn't mean anything by it! I was just saying --"

"Yeah, I know," she cut him off. "How *tired* I look. How very flattering. Thank you."

She dropped the flowers onto the countertop and turned the faucet handle with a vicious twist. Ben's eyes widened and he took another small step backward.

"My God!" Penelope raged while she tore the flowers from their cellophane wrapper. "Is this actually what we've come to?"

Ben stood stone still and silent. He was at a loss as to how he should respond. Besides, she seemed to be talking to herself, not him.

"Truth be told, I've actually had a pretty long day, if you must know."

She thrust the flowers into the vase, filled it with water and thumped it onto the countertop. Ben winced.

"Not necessarily tiring, per se, but, still, long."

Penelope picked up her knife and placed a hand on the celery. Instead of chopping, she began to gesture with the knife, stabbing at the air as she spoke. Ben took yet another small step backward.

"Foolishly," she said, pointing the knife in his direction. "I had the idea that we'd share a nice stir fry, maybe some wine."

Ben blinked, scratched at the blonde stubble on his chin and tried to keep up with her train of thought. He had a strong feeling he was missing some key components that remained unspoken.

"*But*," Penelope practically spat before, much to Ben's relief, she traded her knife for a spatula. "I see now that that was an absurd thing to think. Especially when I *look so bloody tired*!"

Ben took a tentative step forward and tried to place a hand on her shoulder. He had barely grazed the surface of her t-shirt when she shrugged him off.

"Pen," he pleaded and dropped his hand listlessly to his side. "Hang on. I don't know what has happened here, but, let's start over --"

"What would be the point?" She turned sharply to face him. "As I just asked, is *this* how it's going to be?"

Ben had absolutely no idea to what she was referring. However, Penelope was ready to fill him in, in a fast hurry.

"Me, the boring housewife and you, the cliché husband? And, for the love of God, we're not even married yet!"

Ben's eyebrows shot up. Where the hell had that come from?

Penelope pulled the wok off of the hot burner and slapped her spatula into his hand. "Here, you finish this. Maybe you have the appetite for it. Suddenly, I'm not very hungry."

Ben watched, bewildered, as she pushed past him and marched out of the kitchen. He didn't think he could to be more perplexed than he was at that moment.

He sighed, looked at the spatula in one hand; his beer in the other. "Well, nuts," he muttered, then brought the bottle to his lips and drank half of it in one go.

Whatever was going on, he thought, placing both items onto the kitchen table, he needed to get his wits about him and figure it out. Quickly. Or else, he had a sinking feeling, he could be facing a lot of meals for one.

Grayson kissed Cameron lightly on his cool forehead and felt a tug at his heart as he watched his little boy sleep. He was sure that tomorrow would be a better day.

He tiptoed silently out of the boy's bedroom, left the door open a few inches in case he needed them in the night, and made his way downstairs and into the kitchen.

Kris smiled at him when he walked into the room, the phone tucked between her ear and shoulder as she spooned cookie batter onto waiting baking trays.

"Hang on a sec, Renee," Kris said into the phone and then turned to Grayson. "How is he?"

"Much better. I think the bath definitely helped, he's out like a light."

Kris nodded and sighed, relieved. It had been a very long day and the night was shaping up to be calm. Thank goodness.

"You do have a headset, you know," Grayson stated and glanced around the cluttered kitchen. He didn't know how Kris worked in such chaos, but, she seemed to flow through it without a problem. "Somewhere."

Kris put down her spoon and nodded. "I know, but, I'm almost done, so, it's fine."

Grayson smiled. "Okay, well, I'll be in the office if you need me."

Kris picked up a pan and placed it in the oven. Her back was turned, so she missed seeing Grayson stick his head back into the kitchen to steal a cookie from her last batch. She had no idea that he heard the next part of her conversation.

"I know it sounds awful and I sound like a broken record," she said to Renee. "But, sometimes I think I'm going to have to start drinking, just to get through another day of the same routine!"

She slid baked cookies from their trays onto racks and laughed. "Either that, or I'll have to start hanging around the school, like Pen, scouting for gorgeous Single Dads!"

Grayson ducked around the corner into the hallway, so startled by her statement that he almost choked on the warm cookie in his mouth. Never before one to eavesdrop, he stopped dead in his tracks to listen.

"What?" Kris paused and leaned against the granite countertop. "Are you kidding me? So, he actually met the guy? Oh-my-God, I can't imagine what Pen was thinking!"

Grayson frowned and curiosity burned through him. What was she talking about? If only he could hear Renee's side of the conversation.

"Well, be sure to tell me whatever else he says. I should probably call Penelope and hear her side of it."

Grayson leaned against the wall, flummoxed. She could be talking about something, or nothing. He straightened up and was about to tiptoe down the hallway when Kris said something that stopped him in his tracks.

"I have to admit, sometimes I envy her." There was a pause where Grayson had to restrain himself from bursting into the kitchen.

"I know, I know," she said. "Believe me, in my rational moments I tell myself it's just a stage, but ..." Kris took a breath that turned into a yawn.

"Then, I start to panic and ask myself, if this is just a stage, then what's the next one? I'm closing in on forty, for God's sake. Do I ever get a say in it? Or, do I just go along for the ride, until I'm long past forty, no longer needed and, then, when that finally happens, what then?"

Her voice rose in despair and she sat with a creak onto a stool at her kitchen island. "I'll have nothing to fall back on, Renee. Nothing. I'll be middle aged, bored and *boring* --"

Grayson strained to hear her final words and then realized she'd fallen silent, listening to Renee's response. He rubbed his forehead, distressed for his wife. He knew that she was feeling the strain of her every day routine, that much was obvious. However, he had also been under the impression that she was getting a handle on it. Especially when he had tried to talk with her about working for him and she had turned him down, flat.

Grayson walked carefully across the remaining hallway to his office, mindful of squeaking floorboards. The very last thing that he needed was Kris knowing that he'd overheard her, especially when he needed time to think.

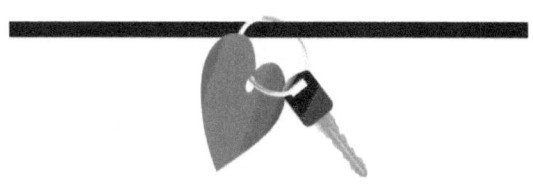

Two

Sunlight crept into Penelope's bedroom through a space between the window curtains. She rolled over beneath her sheets and the shaft of light crossed her face, making her squint.

"Too early," she muttered as she turned her head and buried her face into her pillow.

What a night. She had tossed and turned and finally fallen into a deep sleep sometime in the early morning hours. She had no idea of when Ben had settled in beside her and, judging from his absence, he had decided to clear out early. The space beside her was empty; the only sign that he had been there, was the dent in his pillow.

Penelope sighed and fluffed the pillow under her head. She didn't blame Ben for leaving before she woke up. She had been so angry the previous evening, she, too, would have given herself a wide berth, had she been in his position.

So, she asked herself as she straightened her pajama top, what had made her so angry? Mulling their conversation over in her head, she came to the conclusion that it was the routine, the normalcy, the predictability that had made her nuts.

Penelope threw off her covers and sat on the edge of the bed. She was perplexed. Since when had she been troubled by those things? Hadn't she, in fact, always sought out the comforts of routine? Yes, she confirmed, she had.

"So," she spoke out loud to her bedroom. "Why, then, am I feeling so stuck in a rut that I want to run screaming around the house? That's not normal. And, neither is talking to yourself."

Penelope ran her hands through her sleep-crazed curls and groaned. She had, in the space of one day, become an over reactive loony and was talking, out loud, to herself. The puzzle pieces of her life were seriously out of kilter and she was not enjoying the picture that they were forming - not one bit. Instead of showing her happily ever after, they were revealing to her a landscape that involved another man.

Scott Harrison.

Damn it, Penelope inwardly fumed. Everything had been fine until he'd crossed her path. At least, she had thought things were fine. She massaged her scalp with her fingertips. She was feeling as though she didn't know truth from fiction and wanted to crawl out of her own skin.

The telephone on her bedside table rang shrilly and Penelope jumped. Who could that be? God, she hoped it wasn't her Mother. She really was in no mood to deal with the woman. Penelope cleared her throat and waited a beat to answer, when the phone went silent.

"Penelope?" Ben called from downstairs. "Phone's for you. Can you pick up?"

Penelope rubbed at her sleep creased face. "Yes," she called back and reached tentatively for the receiver. "Hello?"

"Hey," Kris said, as Ben hung up the kitchen extension. "It's me."

Penelope exhaled in relief and tucked herself back under her duvet. "Oh, thank goodness. Hi."

"You okay?"

Penelope chuckled. "Yeah, I'm fine. I was just fretting that it might be my Mother and I am in no mood to deal with her right now."

"What's wrong?"

"Ben and I had an argument, sort of, last night. I'm not sure if it's something, or nothing, but, you know my Mom ..."

"Oh, was it because of that guy?" Kris asked casually.

Penelope sat up. "What?"

"That guy, Single Dad, that you met at the school? Renee told me that you were with him and ran into Paul --"

"Oh, God!" Penelope rubbed her forehead.

"What? What did I say?"

"Did Paul tell Grayson? Did Grayson tell Ben?"

"Okay, back up," Kris said. "I'm lost."

"Has Grayson said anything? Has he spoken to Ben and told him?"

"Told him *what?*"

Penelope threw off her covers and began to pace the hardwood floor of her bedroom. "I don't know! Whatever Paul told him?"

"Okay, first," Kris said. "Grayson didn't say anything to me, it was Renee that told me about Paul meeting you and Single Dad. As for Gray, I'm fairly certain that he knows nothing at all about it."

Penelope stopped pacing. "That's good. So, most likely, Paul only told Renee that he saw me with Scott and, God willing, she patted down the whole thing."

"Pen," Kris asked. "What's going on?"

"Going on?"

"Yes, you're going way over the top and acting like you're guilty of something." Kris paused for a beat. "Are you?"

Penelope sighed and sat on edge of her bed. "No, of course not. I just got really freaked out yesterday when I saw Paul. He looked so thunderous, all serious and over-protective in his business suit and his scowl ..."

"Sounds like Paul," Kris offered. "He is protective."

"I know," Penelope agreed. "But, seriously, you should have seen him. He was worse than usual. His whole demeanor made me feel guilty as hell, even though I hadn't done anything."

Kris wasn't sure how to respond. In her experience she had found that, regardless of whether or not a person had actually done anything, if he, or she, felt guilty, they had a reason. It usually stemmed from thoughts, or desires, that weren't necessarily above board and, then, just like that, guilt surfaced. How to explain that to Penelope, without putting her on the defense, Kris had no idea.

"What makes it worse is," Penelope went on. "I was all wigged out by Paul's reaction and brought that home. Then, Ben came home and was so ... *himself*, that I went off the deep end."

"Himself? What does that mean?"

Penelope shrugged her shoulders. "You know, at this point, even I'm not sure. All I know is, we ended up in a huge argument and, since I haven't spoken to him since last night, it still hasn't been resolved."

"What are you saying?" Kris asked, alarmed. Maybe she and Renee hadn't been jumping the gun in their speculations. "You guys aren't --"

"What?"

"I mean, you guys are going to be okay, right? You're not splitting up, or anything?"

"No, no," Penelope assured her. "Of course not. I'm sure we'll get it worked out. It was a misunderstanding. We'll be fine."

"Can I be honest for a second?"

"Of course."

"You really don't sound fine. You sound like you're still pissed off."

"God!" Penelope exploded, needing no further encouragement. "He just makes me nuts, sometimes!"

"Right. Clearly, *not okay*." Kris commented. "So, what actually happened?"

It's not really just one thing. It's like a combination of things." Penelope tucked her hair behind her ears. "And, they all come together to one spot. *The same. The usual*. Routine --"

"Really?" Kris asked. "This is the first you've even talked about it. I know that you guys have been together for a while --"

"Together for five years, engaged for three," Penelope threw in.

"Right, but, I've never picked up any sort of strong rut vibe from the two of you."

"Well, it turns out there is and the reason you never noticed is because I don't think I've ever really faced it until now."

"Now?"

Penelope sighed. "I don't know. It's like I suddenly woke up and realized that Ben and I are dangerously close to living the life I left behind at home. That was one of the primary reasons that I moved and it's really unsettling to think I may be living it, anyway."

Kris kept silent, again. She didn't think that that was it, at all. Penelope's sudden awakening was too conveniently placed right after her encounter with Single Dad. She may not have seen it, but, Kris was willing to bet that he was the catalyst for Penelope's feelings.

Penelope elaborated. "God, when I think of it, everything staying exactly the same, set in stone, my skin crawls. It was like there was a clear cut path that I was supposed to follow, right along behind my two sisters, into a safe career, a so-so marriage, secure home, blah, blah, blah."

"And those things are bad, because --?"

"They're not *bad*, obviously." Penelope traced an outline around the sliver of sunlight on her bed, with her finger. "I just want to make sure I'm actually making choices, you know? Actually choosing the career, not to mention the guy ..."

"Oh, right," Kris snapped her fingers. "I remember. You had that guy you dated from high school."

Penelope exhaled sharply, remembering. "More than dated, we were briefly engaged."

She allowed herself a moment to recall the boy, Rob. They had been so young, only 19. She had started dating him in her second year of high school and Rob had seamlessly become as much a member of the family as any of them.

He was 'perfect' by her family's standards - handsome, athletic, and he had a promising, stable future ahead of him in his family's auto body shop. Penelope had fit perfectly into the picture, at least from both her family and Rob's viewpoints. Her own perspective; however, had been quite different.

While she had cared about Rob, Penelope had had the sinking feeling that it was a relationship built from habit, instead of love. She had wanted to broach the subject with him, but, then, Rob had proposed, at a baseball game at their local stadium, and Penelope felt she had no choice but to accept. She hadn't wanted to make a fool of Rob. She had also held the youthful notion that, if they were engaged, her feelings would settle down and she'd be content.

It never happened. If anything, she had immediately become more and more unsettled and, very quickly, knew that she had to right her very big wrong.

Rob had been devastated. Penelope had felt terrible. When her family had stepped into the middle and tried to 'fix' things, it all went from bad to worse. Finally, when the last straw had been added by her younger sister, Jennifer - she had discovered that Rob had been unfaithful to Penelope for the entire last year of their relationship - Penelope knew she had to leave.

Not just Rob, the liar that he was, but, her hometown and all of the restrictive thinking it entailed.

She had to get out and establish herself, her way, without a bunch of people who had her pigeon holed from the time she had started talking.

"Did I know this, about you being engaged?" Kris asked, ending Penelope's trip down memory lane.

"I think so. Maybe. I'm not sure." Penelope replied. "But, that's really not the crux of things. The most disturbing thing, the thing that sort of haunts me is, I think if I would have stayed there, I probably would have ended up with that boy. Taken the easy way out." Penelope shook her head. "It sounds awful, but, you get what I mean."

Kris, on the other end of the line, nodded. "I do. I know people, friends, who did that."

"And, their marriages?"

"Done. Divorced. Or, just really distant from each other."

"Exactly." Penelope stated. "That's what I'm saying. I didn't want that. If I had stayed with Rob, that would have been me. But, now, after the argument with Ben, I'm starting to wonder, did I do it anyway and take the easy way out with him, instead?"

Kris didn't immediately reply. She was so surprised by this new revelation, she didn't know how to respond. She had never thought that there was a chance that Penelope was with Ben out of convenience, but, suddenly, it seemed a very valid question. She didn't know which way to turn, toward damage control, or not …

"No," Kris said, finally, treading lightly. "You and Ben? Like that?"

"Obviously, we're not exactly like that. But, the signs of it are there. We've fallen into a rut. A day-by-day, same-old-same-old, routine. And, it's scaring the hell out of me."

Penelope exhaled, suddenly spent. "I thought I left that behind, Kris. I think I may need to do something, to prove to myself that I have actually grown. That I've really moved on from that point in my life."

"Okay, fair enough," Kris said, trying to buy some time and keep any absolutes from their conversation. "What are you thinking?"

"Something *different*. Something that gets my blood pumping."

Kris cringed. She didn't want to go there, into that conversation. If it held reference to Single Dad ... Oh, boy. It was definitely time to go for damage control. "Right, okay, let's recap. First, we know that you love Ben, right?"

"Right."

"I mean, up until now, you've always thought that you were with him because of love, not habit, right?"

"Of course I love him. That's a given. I wouldn't do that to him, or me."

"Okay, good." Kris was careful to keep the huge wave of relief that flooded over her, from her voice. She honestly didn't have a clue what she would have done if Penelope had said otherwise. "So, love aside, you feel that you're in a rut. You still adore him, just not the rut, right?"

Penelope felt as though she had been winded. She wasn't sure. Instead of thinking that the answer to Kris' question was obvious, she wasn't sure. Good God.

"Pen?"

Penelope bought herself some time and coughed. "Sorry, I'm still in bed. I think I had some fluff in my throat."

"The rut?" Kris sounded worried and Penelope jumped in to pat that down.

"Right. Can't stand the rut."

"Well, then, I've got a solution. I know it's going to sound simplistic, but, what about some shopping?" Kris laughed at the silence that met her ears.

"Before you dismiss it," she said. "Think about it. You feel you're in a rut, so, pull yourself out of it! Go and do some shopping, change things up a bit, maybe buy a few new outfits that make you feel different, do something with your hair and, who knows? It might very well spark something in Ben. You'll have a different vibe going on and he may respond differently to that vibe and, tada, suddenly the two of you are changing things and your rut is nothing worth talking about. Sometimes the smallest things can bring the biggest changes."

Penelope smiled. Kris was kind, trying so hard to keep things light.

"You know," she offered, freeing Kris from the obligation of feeling that she needed to solve the problem. "You're probably right."

"Of course I am!"

Penelope laughed. "Retail therapy probably would be a very good thing. Start with me and then let the other stuff start shifting around me."

"That's what I'm saying."

"Okay, I'll do some serious thinking about it." She dropped back against her pillow and propped the phone comfortably against her head. "Now you go."

"Me?"

"I'm assuming you actually called for a reason, besides hearing me bitch?"

"Oh," Kris chuckled. "Yes, but, nothing all that Earth shattering. I was just wanting to thank you, again, for taking care of the boys yesterday."

"Oh, it was nothing. Are you sure?"

"Yes. Totally. I'm thinking of starting a book club."

"I'll join."

Kris laughed. "You're on. I'll let you know when I get it all going."

Penelope grinned. "Excellent. We both have plans. How's Cameron doing?"

"Way better. He's on the upswing now. Although," she paused and sneezed, loudly.

"Bless you."

"Thanks, I've been doing that all morning. I really hope I'm not getting what Cam had."

"Listen," Penelope said, hoping she wasn't been too abrupt. She was finding it difficult to focus and keep up the small talk. Her mind kept on drifting and she needed time to herself to think. "I'm going to go and find Ben."

"Good idea," Kris sniffled. "You guys just need to talk it out some more. You're exactly like me and Grayson."

Penelope raised an eyebrow. She seriously doubted that. Kris and Grayson, even after ten years together, still couldn't keep their hands off of each other.

"You really sound like you could use some rest." Penelope said, side stepping Kris' comment.

Kris sniffled, again, into the phone. Behind the sniffles, Penelope could hear the boisterous arrival of Kyle and Kevin, followed closely by Cameron.

"You're probably right," Kris agreed, raising her voice to be heard over the chatter of her sons. "As you can probably hear, the peanut gallery has arrived in my bedroom."

Penelope laughed. "Well, get them off to school with Grayson and try to take it easy."

Kris blew her nose, causing Penelope to reflexively hold the phone away from her ear. "No way, K," she said, by way of reply.

Penelope waited.

"Put the remote back and take your brothers downstairs for breakfast. Cameron, you're at home with Mommy today."

She coughed and turned her focus back to Penelope. "Sorry about that, Pen. I guess I should go and get them some breakfast."

"No problem, I'll talk to you later," Penelope replied.

"Have a good day."

Penelope hung up and pulled her pajama shirt over her head. The phone began to ring, again, and she left it. She just *knew* that it was her Mother. Who else, besides Kris, would call so early?

A perk! She suddenly thought, with a laugh, as she walked into her en-suite. The routine that they were in was providing a positive benefit. Perhaps not for Ben, who had to take the call, but, still ...

Penelope turned the tap for the shower, stepped inside and pulled the curtain closed. Maybe, she'd get an additional benefit and her Mother would be the catalyst to inspire Ben to vacate the house before she was even done with her shower. That way, she thought, with fingers crossed, she wouldn't have to deal with him at all.

"Knock, knock?" Penelope gently pushed open Renee's door and poked her head into the kitchen. "Anybody home?"

It was shortly after two in the afternoon and Penelope was counting on having a few minutes with Renee before her family arrived home from school.

"Who's that?" Renee called out from her office.

"It's me," Penelope answered and closed the door behind her.

"Penelope?" Renee questioned as she walked down the hallway into her kitchen with Poppy, their scrappy Yorkshire Terrier, prancing behind.

"Oh, dear," Penelope said, when she saw Renee. "You're busy, I'm intruding."

Renee was dressed in what she called her work uniform - yoga pants and an oversized, man's dress shirt. She managed to make it look cute, rolling up the sleeves to elbow length and wearing a tank-top underneath so that she only had to button it half way. Combined with her short, black hair and bright, blue eyes, she looked bohemian, instead of how Penelope knew she would look - sloppy.

"No, you're not. This is just unexpected. Is something wrong?" Renee gave Penelope a quizzical look. "What time is it, anyway? Do you want coffee?"

"You're sure I'm not interrupting?"

"Pah," Renee waved her hand dismissively. "I wasn't doing anything that can't wait."

Penelope grinned and reached down to pat Poppy. "Okay, well, in answer to your question, it's still early, and, yes, coffee would be great, thanks."

Renee pulled lime green cups from a coffee mug tree and picked up her coffee pot. "So, you haven't answered my question. What brings you here, in your work clothes, in the middle of the day?"

Penelope looked down at her navy blue suit. She had ditched work for this. It was time to air out her thoughts. "I've been going through some stuff and I just needed a person to talk to. I was trying to focus at work, but, my thoughts are in a real jumble, so, I decided to call it a day and take off early."

Renee's eyebrows knitted together with concern as she poured their coffee. "Is everything okay? Are you okay? Is it Ben?"

"No," Penelope shook her head. "Nothing serious like that, just my own stuff ... In my head." She took the cup of coffee Renee handed to her. "Thanks."

Renee reached into the pantry for a dog biscuit. "Poppy, to your bed," she said. The small dog tucked herself into her cushy basket and Renee gave her her biscuit. "Good girl," she told the dog and then sat down at the table.

Penelope watched, impressed. She had a hunch that, if she had a dog, it would smirk and ignore her.

"Well, then," Renee gestured at Penelope to take a seat. "Take a load off and start talking."

"I guess I'll jump in feet first," Penelope said as she unfastened the buttons on her jacket and pulled out a chair. "Meeting that single dad - Scott - really did a number on me."

Renee nodded, took a sip of coffee from her cup and settled back into her chair.

"I didn't realize it right at first, but, by the time I got home, especially after seeing him a second time at the school --"

"When you saw Paul, too?"

"Yes. Jeez, Kris told me this morning that he said something. Did he let it drop?"

"Not at first, but, he has now," Renee said.

"Translation?"

"He brought it up last night, at dinner. Then, he let it drop when the girls started listening and asking questions --"

"Oh, hell," Penelope said.

"No, it was fine," Renee assured her. "They were just typical, seven year old questions. Nothing serious. Paul was able to blow them off easily and change the subject."

"So, I don't have to worry about them asking me questions when Ben's around?"

Renee laughed. "I seriously doubt that! Their world is pretty self-centered, Pen. Their Daddy mentioning a friend he met with Auntie Penelope isn't something that they are likely to put at the top of their lists as something to remember."

Penelope smiled. She had a point. "So, that was it? Kris made it sound like a lot more."

"Oh, there was more. Later, after the girls were in bed, Paul quizzed me as to whether or not I," Renee hooked her fingers into air quotes. "'Knew the guy'. His words, not mine."

Penelope cringed. "What did you say?"

"I'd had time to prepare, because of his comments at dinner, so, I blathered on about how you probably knew him from work, that he was probably a client and it was a coincidence that he happened to also have a child at the same school as our kids."

"You patted it down," Penelope stated.

"Exactly."

"Do you think it worked?"

"He's a man, Pen. How many men do you know that belabor every little thing, like a woman?"

Another good point, Penelope thought. Was that what she was doing? Belaboring things and making something out of nothing?

"So, anyway," Renee said. "That aside, you're feeling weird after you saw Single Dad at the school, again?"

Penelope nodded and refocused on her original thoughts. She still wanted to air them out, to see if they had any validity. "Yes. I didn't realize how much it had stirred up inside of me, until I went home. I had a chance to think on it, while I was preparing dinner and it was like, whoosh! Clarity. A sudden, crystal clear, view of my life."

"Meaning?"

"Meaning ... I saw my life from a different perspective and I did not like the view I was seeing."

Renee nodded, thoughtful. "What perspective?"

"It was as though I'd stepped back, and could see the big picture, and it wasn't what I thought it was."

"What did you think it was?"

"I guess," Penelope shrugged. "I thought Ben and I had this cozy, comfortable thing going on and, in reality, we have something that is routine, same old, same old and ... safe."

Renee looked at Penelope with genuine concern. This was serious. She had to tread carefully. "I always thought safe was a good thing."

Penelope leaned her elbows on the table and rested her chin in her hands. "Of course it is, but, this sort of safe isn't. There's no heat, Renee."

Renee looked surprised and Penelope sat back, wide eyed that she'd voiced her thoughts. "There," she blurted. "I said it and I can't take it back. I know a person isn't supposed to kiss and tell, but, too late. I said it."

Renee couldn't help herself and snickered. She raised her voice an octave and said, "Oooh, you're bad!"

Penelope rolled her eyes and started to laugh. "It's not funny," she said, trying not to smirk.

"No, no, I know it's not." Renee cleared her throat. "I was just trying to lighten things up a bit. But, seriously, Pen, no heat? None, whatsoever?"

"No," Penelope shook her head.

Renee looked at her, skeptical.

"Okay, fine. There might be *some*, but --"

"Just not the, knock-your-socks-off, make-your-stomach-lurch, variety that you felt when you set eyes on Single Dad."

Penelope had the good grace to blush.

"Uh-huh, that's what I thought," Renee said, nodding her head, knowingly. "But, you do realize that the so-called heat you felt around that guy, was not on a scale that can be compared to real life, right?"

Penelope slouched back into her seat and pulled the hairpins from her scalp. Her curls burst from their confines and fell around her face in a haphazard manner, as though emphasizing her state of mind.

"I guess," she said. "It was just so unexpected that, afterward, everything else suddenly became really, really lackluster by comparison."

"Well, of course it did!" Renee insisted, throwing her hands into the air. "You said that the guy was beyond gorgeous and he fawned all over you."

"He really was. He could wear BCGs and make them look good."

Renee frowned. "BCGs?"

Penelope grinned. "Yeah, you know, BCGs. Birth control glasses. Those thick, black, horned rimmed glasses that so many people - mostly celebrities - have taken to wearing and think that they're attractive enough to wear them, when, in reality, they are so not."

Renee burst out laughing.

"So," Penelope said. "Now you know how attractive Scott is, if he could wear BCGs and still look gorgeous."

Renee got a hold of herself and shook her head. "Well, if that's the case, then how on Earth could anything really compete with that?"

Penelope shrugged.

"*Unless*," Renee leaned forward, hoping to make a point. "You have something deeper in your relationship. Something richer that resonates to a different part of your being. Something that no amount of superficial, physical zing can compare to."

Penelope knew that Renee was speaking from her own experience with Paul. Those two were deep down in their commitment. Taking that as her example, Penelope wondered, could she really say that her relationship with Ben held the same bond?

"What are you thinking?" Renee asked as she watched a myriad of emotions flit across Penelope's face.

"I'm thinking that, I'm so all over the place, I honestly have no idea what the hell I think. I truly thought that Ben and I had something deeper, but, then, when Scott materialized --"

"He's just a guy, Pen." Renee spoke softly, but, firmly. It was time to put Single Dad into perspective.

"Yes, he's gorgeous," Renee acknowledged. "Yes, he's charming. But, when all that settles down into the dust, so what? There are lots of attractive, charming men who will never be able to go the distance. Ben, on the other hand, is one of the rare ones who will. He's very attractive, not to mention kind, charming, generous. The list goes on. Most importantly, he loves you enough for both of you."

Penelope stayed quiet and listened. Renee was right. She knew that. However, correct or not, Penelope had to face the question that loomed in her mind ...

Did she want to spend the rest of her life with someone who loved her enough for both of them, or with someone *she* loved enough for both of them?

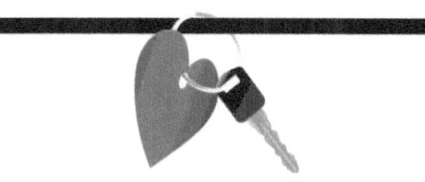

THREE

Penelope took a deep breath and stepped tentatively across the threshold of the posh salon. She could not believe that she had decided to follow Kris' advice. It seemed so superficial, but, at least she was doing something to get the ball rolling - hopefully, in the right direction. Maybe, a new look would be just what she needed to stop her from blaming Ben for her feelings of being trapped in a never ending cycle of sameness. It was worth a try.

Penelope looked around the salon and felt like the proverbial doe in the headlights. Everything she looked at, from the gleaming granite countertop of the reception desk, to the multitudes of decorative glass and mirrors on the walls, seemed to sparkle at her. In her no nonsense, navy blue suit, she felt drab and colorless by comparison.

Maybe she'd made a mistake asking Kris for the name of her stylist and should have just gone to her regular place ... a Mega-Cuts discount salon, close to home.

"Hello! Welcome!" A pretty blonde, all sequins and lip gloss, popped up from behind the imposing rock and glass desk and gushed at Penelope. "You must be Penelope, yes?"

Penelope nodded, and, then, silently cursed that she hadn't turned tail and ran before she was spotted. "Is it that obvious?" She attempted to joke.

"I'm sorry?" the girl cocked her head to one side and blinked her long, had to be fake, eyelashes.

"Oh, it's nothing," Penelope grinned and attempted to explain. "It's just that everything's so sparkly, I figured that, by contrast, I probably stand out like a sore thumb."

"Oh!" The girl's green eyes widened and she shook her sheet of blonde hair. "No, no! Please don't think like that!" She stood up and clutched her hands to her impressive cleavage. "It's just that I know most of our clients, and this is your first time here, so I knew --"

"Right," Penelope cut in, sorry for having to make her explain. "Of course. That makes perfect sense. So, anyway, I have an appointment with Monique."

The girl beamed at her and gestured to her computer screen. Penelope hadn't even noticed it, discreetly tucked into the corner of the desk. "Yes, you're right here," she pointed. "However, I'm sorry to tell you that Monique has called in sick."

"Oh," Penelope frowned. Why had she not been informed, before she had traveled to the salon?

"You're probably wondering why I didn't call you and reschedule, right?"

"Well, actually, yes, I am --"

"Because, I have wonderful news!" The girl clapped her hands with glee. Penelope took a small step back, slightly overwhelmed by the woman's enthusiasm.

"It turns out that Bosco *is* available to step in for Monique, to help achieve your new styling ideals."

Bosco? Penelope thought, with a hint of amusement. Styling ideals? That would be wonderful, *if* she actually had any. Truth be told, she had been counting upon Monique to help her out in that department. Instead, she had *Bosco*. Huh.

"Well, okay, that sounds just fine," Penelope agreed, when she realized that the girl was eagerly awaiting her response. "And, thanks for fitting me in on such short notice."

"Oh, no trouble at all!" She winked and leaned forward eagerly, as though she was a sharing a secret. "As soon as I heard your voice, I *knew* it was going to be a challenge."

Penelope raised an eyebrow. Really, she thought, I came across as a challenge? Just from my voice?

"That's why I put the bug in Bosco's ear."

"Oh, well," Penelope stammered. "I wasn't wanting anything too terribly drastic. I could have waited for Monique --"

The girl waved her hand dismissively. "No problem. When Monique called in sick, I knew that it was destiny. If there's one thing that Bosco loves, it's a challenge."

Penelope smiled, weakly.

The girl winked, again, and stepped out from behind her desk. Penelope could not believe how tiny her waist was, considering the impressiveness of her chest.

"Follow me," she said, and led Penelope to Bosco's chair. It was hard to miss. It was a deep burgundy, the only one in a sea of black, and monogrammed. "Can I get you a coffee, while you wait? An espresso? Latte?"

"Um," Penelope thought. "I guess, if that's okay, a Latte would be wonderful. Thank you."

"No problem! Make yourself comfortable and I'll be right back."

Penelope sat down in Bosco's burgundy leather chair and goggled at his work station. It was as though she'd entered into another dimension. Everything, from the polished rock counter top, to the brushes, combs and hair products, gleamed. She wondered if he had a personal assistant, just to attend to his stuff. All around his gilt framed mirror, he had pictures tacked up of … himself? They were Warhol-esk in nature, some close up in black and white, others with repetitive shots in primary colors, and, still more, with props like hats, or, fruit, or, bizarrely shaped sunglass. Put together, they created a collage so oddly compelling, that Penelope felt she was almost being dared to pull her eyes away.

"Darling!"

Penelope jumped in her seat.

"Let's get this project started!"

Penelope whipped her head around and her jaw went slack. A gorgeous, slim, razor-sharp-cheek-boned, man stood framed, in a well-disguised doorway, at the side of the salon. Penelope had thought it was a wall, but, clearly she had been mistaken.

Bosco, she thought. There was no questioning it was him, she had been staring at his photos for the past five minutes. They didn't do him justice.

"He's here!" Blonde, perky receptionist gushed as she clicked across the floor in her impossibly high heels, Penelope's Latte held aloft in front of her generous chest.

Penelope blinked and felt as though she was on the sidelines of a movie set, watching as the man sashayed across the floor, the multitude of overhead lights causing him to twinkle.

Where, Penelope wondered, were these stunning men coming from, all of a sudden? First that Scott guy, now *Bosco*. Although, admittedly, Scott's good looks were masculine, whereas Bosco's leaned way to the side of beautiful.

In fact, if Penelope was truthful, she would admit that she didn't just admire him, she wanted to be like him. His golden skin was flawless, his short, butter-blonde hair was cut to display the perfect contours of his head, his sea green eyes sparkled, she could have watched him all day.

"So, Darling," Bosco shimmered at her when he arrived at his personalized chair. "You are in desperate need of a transformation, yes?"

Penelope attempted to find her voice while he cast a critical eye at her head. "A transformation? Well, no, that's not what I was thinking when I came in."

"No?" He pouted, prettily.

"But," Penelope amended. "If I could end up looking like you, then, what the hell, yes! Transform me!"

Bosco threw his head back and laughed. His energy was infectious and Penelope found herself laughing with him. She could not believe she had said what was in her thoughts, out loud!

"Well, my lovely flower," he patted her head affectionately. "While certainly flattering, I don't think you really want to look like me. No, no. Just a more polished and perfect version of yummy you!"

Penelope giggled. She had never thought of herself as 'yummy', but, if that's what Bosco thought, she'd buy it. Heck, just looking at him made her want to buy whatever he was selling!

"So, we definitely need to cut, yes?" Bosco lifted strands of her hair and let them drop as he tilted his head this way and that way, getting the full picture of what was before him.

"And, a color, of course!" He glanced at the perky receptionist, who placed the Latte on the counter and nodded as though it couldn't be more obvious. "You see? Even Brooke knows! We cannot create half way, darling. It's all the way, or nothing!"

Penelope found herself joining in and nodding enthusiastically. She had only intended to get a trim, but, suddenly, that seemed so *boring*. "All the way," she reiterated and sat up straighter in the chair. "It has to be done."

Bosco clapped his hands. So did Brooke.

"Magnificent!" He declared. "Oh, we're going to have such fun, my Buttercup! Let's get started!"

Penelope beamed as he produced a magenta colored cape - seemingly out of nowhere -whipped it around her shoulders with a flourish and gallantly offered her his arm. She stood up, dazzled, and allowed him to lead her off to the sinks.

"Okay, girls," Renee instructed Alexa and Zoe. "That looks mixed enough. Now, working as a team, one of you holds the bowl and the other scrapes the batter into the pan."

Paul looked up from the laundry he was folding to watch. The twin's faces mirrored each other as they concentrated. He was impressed, they were even ignoring Poppy as she danced around the bottom of their chairs, looking for attention.

"I really think it would be a good thing for you to call both of your brothers and arrange a guy's night out," Renee said as she hovered around her daughters and wiped at the counter top, trying to look as though she wasn't hovering.

Paul folded a purple towel and placed it on top of his growing pile of clothes. "Something I should know first?"

Renee glanced at her daughters, to make sure that they were still focused on their task, and scooped Poppy up into her arms. "Well, when I spoke to Kris, she seemed really stressed. I'm thinking that if she's stressed, probably Grayson is, too. And, as for Penelope, she stopped over here this afternoon --"

"She wasn't at work?"

"She was, but, she took a half day."

Paul frowned and folded another purple towel. "So, she took the day off to shuttle the boys, made friendly with some Dad guy and then, today, took a half day?"

Renee rolled her eyes. So much for her big talk to Penelope about how men don't hold onto things like women.

"I don't get that," Paul huffed, his face screwed up in annoyance.

"*She's just needing some time to herself,*" Renee spoke through clenched teeth and indicated, with short jerks of her head, their two daughters. "*Little pitchers...*"

Paul looked at Renee, registered her irritation and dropped his attitude. He wasn't a lawyer for nothing. "Right," he nodded, affecting a much more casual tone. "Nothing strange there at all."

"Anyway," Renee said, cutting her eyes at him. She was no dummy, either. "I'm just saying, an outing with your brothers might be a good thing."

"Okay, I'm sure you're right." Paul kept his voice neutral, quitting while he still had a chance of being ahead. "I haven't talked to Gray for a bit, or Ben, for that matter. Sounds like a plan."

Renee nodded, satisfied, and stoked the top of Poppy's little head. The Yorkie twisted her body around to lick affectionately at Renee's chin.

"Good job, girls!" She praised her daughters as they finished spreading cake batter like a couple of miniature pros.

"We learned from watching you, Mommy," Alexa said, all smiles as she wiped her hands on the flower speckled apron around her tiny waist.

Zoe nodded her agreement. "You're the best cake maker, Mommy, so we should be good at it, too, right?"

"Bang on," Paul said as he folded the last towel. "You'll be taking over for Mommy in no time."

Renee grinned and he winked at her.

"Now it goes into the oven, right?" Alexa asked, her eyes bright with anticipation. Watching the cake batter rise was her favorite part. It was like magic.

"Correct," Renee said and tucked Poppy into her basket in the corner of the room. She quickly rinsed her hands at the sink and then picked up the cake pan from the counter top. "Whose turn is it?"

"Mine," Zoe answered and skipped in little steps across the kitchen to the oven.

"Hands clean?"

Zoe quickly examined her hands, gave them a quick swipe across her ladybug patterned apron and nodded. "Clean."

"Excellent. Ready?"

Zoe pulled on an oven mitt and Renee grinned as it covered her arm, all the way to her elbow.

"Ready," she said, her expression serious as she carefully opened the oven door, then quickly stepped back, just as her Mother had taught her.

Renee waited half a beat as the heat billowed from the oven, then gently slipped the cake pan inside. Zoe stepped forward to firmly close the door and Renee felt as though she was visibly puffing up with pride at her girls.

"Just like a pro, Zo," Paul said as he offered her his hand for a high-five.

"You're a poet and you didn't even know it, Daddy," Alexa piped up, giggling.

"So, you'll call today your brothers, then?" Renee asked.

"I'll do it now, while it's in my head," Paul picked up the laundry basket.

"Frosting, right?" Renee confirmed with her daughters.

"Yes, chocolate!" Alexa enthused as Zoe pulled a jar of cocoa from the cupboard.

Renee blew Paul a kiss and turned her attention to Zoe, before her entire kitchen became sprinkled with a fine dusting of cocoa powder.

"My God," Penelope raved as she stared at herself.

She was in a clothing shop, intent upon starting her retail therapy, but, could not tear her eyes away from her reflection in the mirror. Bosco has transformed her!

Penelope watched as the light danced on her newly colored and styled hair. Gone were the frizzy and wacky curls, and, in their place, soft, shiny, bouncy waves. And, a red head! She had held the secret desire, for as long as she could remember, to have dark auburn hair and Bosco had looked into her mousy brown colored soul, saw that girl and brought her forward. Bless him.

"Can I help you find anything?"

Penelope jumped at the sound of the salesperson's voice. She had to get a grip. "Oh! Sorry, I didn't mean to hog the mirror. I just came from the salon --" she gestured to her head.

"And, you're gorgeous!" The salesgirl affirmed. "That is *so* your color! Whoever did it is a genius!"

Penelope grinned. She liked this girl. "I think so, too. I mean, I didn't know it was my color, until it was done, but, now I do." She took a deep breath and focused. "Anyway, yes, in answer to your question, I would love some help."

"What are you looking for?" The girl quickly skimmed Penelope's form with her eyes and cocked her head, listening closely.

"Well, pretty much everything, if you want the truth."

"Right," The girl said. She narrowed her brown eyes, placed a hand on one of her slim hips, and gave Penelope a deeply appraising gaze. Finally, she nodded. "I feel you."

Penelope looked at the way the girl was dressed, in a high waisted, deep red, pencil skirt and a crisp, white, blouse, complete with French cuffs. Her hair, the color of rich chocolate, was artfully arranged into a low bun at the nape of her neck and the perfect accent to her outfit. She was the epitome of grace and style. Penelope trusted her immediately to guide her through the store.

"We're going to do very well today," the girl grinned.

"Oh, good," Penelope said, relieved to have the burden of choosing alone taken from her shoulders. "Because, I'm not the sort of shape that's off the rack --"

"You are today," the salesgirl stated confidently. "You've got hidden attributes, that much I know. Trust me, you'll be shocked at how much off the rack stuff we'll find that will go perfectly with your gorgeous new hair. We'll make you a whole new woman!"

Penelope restrained herself from clapping with excitement. She felt like Cinderella and followed happily behind her salesgirl/fairy Godmother as she started pulling clothes from racks.

Penelope walked through the coffee shop doors and made a speedy beeline for an available table. She sat down and stacked her numerous bags precariously on an adjacent chair. She was exhausted and needed a coffee.

"Penelope?"

Surprised to hear her name, Penelope turned to find a coworker of Ben's standing beside her table. He was staring at her, his face incredulous.

"Hi," she said. "Todd, isn't it?"

Todd nodded enthusiastically. "Yes! God, I wasn't sure if it was you, but, it is. Wow! You look, umm, so different than I remember!"

"Oh," Penelope nodded.

"What I mean is," Todd elaborated. "You look great. Really fantastic."

"Well, thank you," Penelope smiled. "You, uh, well, you look good, too."

Todd had the good grace to laugh. "Thanks. But, seriously, the last time I saw you - was it at the Autumn party at the office? You definitely had a whole other look going on."

"Yes," Penelope said, at a loss for words. What could she say?

Todd's cheeks took on a light blush as he fell over his own words in hasty clarification. "Not that the other look wasn't, well, you *know*. It was! It's just that, *this*," he waved his hand in her general direction. "This is so *different* --"

Oh, boy, it was painful. Penelope put him out of his misery.

"Thank you, Todd," she said, gently, allowing him to catch his breath and for his color to return to normal. "I just needed a change, so, that's what I did. Changed."

"Well," Todd nodded. "It definitely suits you."

Penelope smiled. "Thanks."

Todd glanced around the coffee shop. "So, is Ben with you?"

"No," Penelope began.

"Oh," He stopped short and his features twisted awkwardly. "Or, uh, are you two --"

"Oh, yes," Penelope cut in, to circumvent another babbling moment, and flashed her engagement ring. "We are definitely still a solid two."

Todd exhaled and looked relieved. "Great! That's just great. Well, I should go --"

"Of course," Penelope nodded.

"I'm sure I'll see Ben at work."

"You bet," Penelope barely managed to reply as Todd sprinted out of the coffee shop. She couldn't help but chuckle. So, she looked fantastic, huh? Well, that was certainly good news.

"Coming!" Kris called, in response to the sound of her doorbell.

She pulled a tissue from a box on her kitchen table and vigorously blew her nose. She was in no mood for visitors and regretted her knee jerk reaction to the bell. She was seriously considering ignoring it, anyway, when it rang a second time. She sighed. Whomever had pressed it the first time, was not going away.

"Alright," Kris sniffled and shuffled, in fluffy, duck shaped slippers - a Mother's Day gift from her boys - into her front hallway.

"Achoo!" She sneezed, explosively, just barely succeeding in covering her mouth and nose with her tissue as she pulled open her front door, "Whew," she exhaled as she wiped her pink nose, then looked up to find ... "Penelope!"

Penelope grinned, thrilled to pieces by the surprised expression on Kris' face. "Bless you!" She blurted, her eyed bright with barely suppressed glee.

Kris stared at her best friend, at a loss for words. It was Penelope and, yet, it wasn't. She looked positively radiant in a chocolate brown, figure hugging skirt; a floaty, animal print blouse that showcased her cleavage;

sparkly, silver earrings dangling from her ears ... Kris had never seen her look so polished.

Penelope waited, watching Kris' reaction. When she didn't say anything, just stared with a stunned, almost frozen expression on her face, Penelope began to feel concerned.

"Are you okay?"

Kris blinked and cleared her throat. "Sure," she said, gripping her tissue as she tightened the sash on her blue, flannel robe. "You just startled me."

"Can I come in?" Penelope finally asked, feeling a bit awkward, standing on the step.

"Oh, God, yes, of course, come in!" Kris stepped aside to let Penelope pass.

Penelope turned on her new, red heels and decided to start over. She squared her shoulders and made an effort to sparkle. "Well?" She said, expectantly. "What do you think?"

Kris leaned against the closed door and took a breath, buying time. There was no question in her mind what she thought. Envy. Pure, ugly and straight to the point.

Envy that Penelope had effortlessly pulled off a huge change. HUGE. Envy that she had done so while she, Kris, couldn't even make the smallest of changes to take back even a corner of her life.

"Monique did THAT?" Kris, finally, spat as she raked her fingers aggressively through her lank, unwashed hair. Her envy both winded and shocked her. It was something that she had so rarely ever felt in her lifetime, she didn't have a clue how to handle it.

Penelope raised an eyebrow at Kris' tone. Why was she acting so strangely? "Actually, no, Monique wasn't in the salon. She called in sick, so ..."

Penelope took a breath. Her words were starting to tumble over themselves. She waited a beat, hoping for a flicker of *something* from Kris. Nothing. Kris just kept on wiping her nose and staring at her newly quaffed head.

Penelope swallowed and continued to fill the silence. "Instead of calling me to reschedule, the receptionist gave my appointment over to another stylist named, wait for it ... Bosco."

She laughed merrily, fully expecting that Kris would join her. Again, nothing. Kris blew her nose and nodded. Tough room.

"Anyway," Penelope said, giving it a final shot. "Bosco turned out to be this hair styling God, and, tada, he made some changes."

"Well, aren't you something," Kris' mouth twisted with barely suppressed envy and her voice sounded shrill, even to her ears. "You wanted to make some changes and, just like that, you did it. No questions, no queries, just like that."

Penelope nodded, tentatively. "You're the first person I've come to show," she said, hoping that if she continued to show excitement, Kris would join her. "Are Grayson and the boys here?"

Kris shook her head and stuffed her hands into her pockets. "No, they went out for dinner to let me have an evening off."

"Well, that's okay. It was you I wanted to see first, anyway. I thought that you'd be the best one to start with, you know? Since we had that talk?"

Kris looked off into the distance and sniffled loudly, not willing to meet Penelope's eye. Something wasn't adding up.

"Or, maybe," Penelope switched tactics, narrowed her eyes and placed a hand on her hip. "I thought wrong?"

Kris, finally, glanced at her, a guilty shadow crossing her face. "No, you weren't wrong. As I said, you just caught me off guard, is all."

"Off guard?"

Kris shuffled past her and dropped gracelessly into a living room chair. "Yes. You surprised me. I just need a moment to get a good look at you. I'm, clearly, not on my A game and, you have to admit, this *is* a ridiculously big change to take in at a moment's notice."

Penelope's jaw dropped. The tone that Kris was giving her sounded a lot like judgment. Was she hearing correctly? "Ridiculously big? What does that mean?"

"It doesn't mean anything. I'm just stating the truth. You did something really drastic, so, give a girl - especially one with a dripping nose and a headache - a chance to catch up."

"The truth?" Penelope curved her fingers into air quotes.

Kris pulled a new tissue from her pocket and blew her nose. "Pen, don't misunderstand me --"

"Don't worry, I don't think I could if I tried," Penelope huffed, hurt and frustrated. "Yes, as a matter of fact, I am aware that what I've done is a large change. Considering, I was the one who did the changing! And, like a fool, I thought that the one person who would be all, 'good for you, Pen', would be you!"

"No, not foolishly," Kris said stiffly, her chin thrust forward. "I remember what we talked about and I do think it's good, it's just this --"

"What, exactly?"

"Let me finish!" Kris stood up and started to pace between the living room and front hallway, her slippers making a thwack, thwack sound with each step.

"I'm saying that this," she gestured at Penelope's transformed hair and wardrobe. "It's a lot. It comes across like you're trying to be something that you're not."

Penelope coughed, her eyes round like saucers. "Excuse me?"

"And," Kris held up her hand, finger pointed in the air. "I'll have you know that I did some serious thinking about what you told me. I'm a bit worried, Pen, that you might be acting out, you know?"

"Acting out?" Penelope frowned. "What am I, ten years old? What does that even mean?"

"Well, It's kind of hard to miss noticing that this sudden need for change, has come on the heels of you meeting Single Dad."

"You have got to be kidding me!" Penelope spat. It was all getting to be too much.

Kris ignored Penelope's anger. "No, I'm not kidding. Single Dad equals you not happy with your life. It all seems to connect. And, I'm just concerned for you, that you might regret your impulsive changes once the flush of meeting him wears off and you come back to your normal self. Not to mention, how will Ben react, if you haven't discussed your decisions with him?"

"What a load of psychological crap! '*Impulsive changes*'," Penelope mocked, her face contorted between hurt and rage. "It sounds like bad daytime talk show babble. But, then, I guess you'd know all about that, right?"

"Hey," Kris said, indignation mottling her features.

Penelope pulled herself up tall, thankful for the new heels that elevated her a few inches closer to Kris' height. "So, I get the guts to make some changes, changes that you know I have wanted to make for a long time."

"Yes, but ---"

"My God," Penelope threw her hands in the air. "We just talked about it. In fact, retail therapy was your damned suggestion in the first place! And, this is the response I get?"

"I didn't suggest THIS!" Kris retorted, waving her hand, dismissively, up and down at Penelope's new outfit and hair. "Don't put the onus on me. I said a bit of a change, a few new outfits. Like you normally wear. Not a complete transformation into a new, God-damned, person!"

Penelope stepped forward and pointed her index finger accusingly at Kris. "You know, I think that, maybe, it's not what Ben will think that's the issue here. Or, for that matter, the whole Single Dad crap."

Kris folded her arms tightly across her chest.

Penelope took a deep breath and finished. "I think this is all about what you think. Maybe, you've got some strange jealously going on. My changes threaten you because you'll no longer hold center stage. God forbid, plain old Penelope might actually have something to offer besides her sense of humor!"

Kris looked stunned and Penelope set her mouth in a firm line. "Well, that's fine. Just fine. I get it. But, just so you know," she said, her voice hard. "I really did think that you, of all people, would be supportive."

When Kris didn't offer any feedback, Penelope turned and opened the front door. "After all," she said. "You're the one who has it all. The house, the kids, the looks, the talent. So, you'd think that you'd be happy for me, just this once, getting even a little bit of my own."

Kris watched as Penelope stalked down her front path, her new heels giving a seriously sexy swing to her hips. She got behind the wheel of a shiny, red car that Kris didn't recognize, and Kris wondered to whom it belonged. Hunky Single Dad?

Kris wanted so very badly to call out to Penelope, beg her to come back so that they could work it all out. But, she didn't. She couldn't. All she could do was watch her peel away from the curb and go back inside to ask herself the question, was Penelope right?

"Okay, Kris, you need to calm down," Renee said, into the phone. She reached into her cupboard for a pink, plastic cup and handed it to Zoe. "We can get this worked out. You and Penelope both said some stuff in haste, but, I really think we can get this handled."

Zoe, standing on a yellow, step stool, placed the cup on the countertop in front of her and reached for the juice jug. She carefully poured her juice, while Poppy danced around her legs, looking for attention.

"We both know that Penelope is pretty," Renee said as she gave a thumbs-up signal to her daughter. "Always has been. She was the one who never saw it."

Zoe picked up her cup, took a long swallow and then carefully made her way out of the room, Poppy on her heels.

"I think," Renee went on, as she returned the container to her fridge. "If you'll grant me the liberty of saying so, your reaction to Pen was based on your own stuff. Have you even discussed with her how you've been feeling this past while?"

She waited a beat for Kris' reply. "Right, I didn't think so. Because, I really think that you wouldn't have felt so much need to slam what she's done --"

Renee paused as Kris interrupted, then continued. "Okay, fine, perhaps 'slam' her was too strong, but, you get what I mean. Your reaction, I think, came from a place of feeling stuck in your own ruts and Penelope's changes just brought that racing to the forefront."

There was a firm knock at her door and Renee looked up, surprised, to see the Penelope's blurred image through the frosted glass. Her face, on the other side of the pane, was set in a rigid expression. Renee sighed. Oh, boy.

"Listen, Kris," Renee interrupted Kris' rambling as she walked across the kitchen to unlock the door. "Penelope is at my door, so --"

"Is that her?" Penelope insisted as she stormed past Renee into the kitchen. "That's Kris, right?"

Renee's eyes widened in disbelief. This was a whole new Penelope. Kris had been right on the money; her transformation was both drastic and beautiful.

Renee held up a hand, hoping to insert calm into the situation. "Yes, it's Kris," she replied and then spoke, again, into the phone. "Kris, clearly you can hear it's Pen. I'm going to call you back, okay?"

Penelope slumped into a chair at the table, annoyance twisting her features while she waited for Renee to hang up the phone. The moment Renee pressed the 'end' button, she launched her attack. "Did she tell you what happened? The truth?"

"I think so," Renee replied, her voice steady and soothing. "But, you tell me as well, so that I have both points of view, okay?"

Penelope's face relaxed. Renee wasn't immediately taking sides. "Okay."

Renee nodded and sat down in the chair beside Penelope. "Good. You look absolutely beautiful, by the way."

Penelope's face crumpled. "Thank you." She started to sniffle and Renee patted her shoulder. "That's all I was hoping for, you know. Just a little bit of, 'Hey, good for you, Pen'. I wasn't expecting over-the-top gushing. Just the support of a friend."

Renee nodded and patted, her petite features pulled together in concern. "I know, I know. And, we do support you --"

"No!" Penelope sniffled, her voice petulant. "Not, we."

"Yes, we," Renee affirmed, ignoring Penelope's insistence. "It's just that, sometimes, when the people you love make big changes," she gestured to Penelope's transformation. "It can take us off guard and we have to sort of regroup to keep up."

Penelope pulled a tissue from her jacket pocket and wiped her nose. "What needs regrouping? How can my changes, in any way, affect her life?"

Renee sighed. Time, once again, for damage control. She stood up and walked over to the cupboard. "Do you want some tea? Maybe chamomile? And, some cookies?"

Penelope nodded as the telephone rang. "Do you want me to get that for you?"

"No, I've got it," Renee reached for the phone. "Hello? Oh, hi --"

Renee's tone alerted Penelope, and she stared intently. "Who is it?"

When Renee paused, something in Penelope snapped. "It's her, again, isn't it?!"

Renee opened her mouth to respond, but, Penelope cut her off, furious.

"Not fair, Kris!" She yelled.

"Penelope!" Renee admonished.

Penelope ignored her and continued to shout. "Not fair, at all! I get to have my moment to say my side, too! You don't get every damned moment!"

Paul stuck his head into the kitchen. "Hey, everything okay?" He looked from Renee to Penelope, then lifted his eyebrows in surprise at Penelope. "Wow, Pen, look at you."

Renee frowned, Paul was definitely not helping. She pointed a finger at Penelope, much as she would one of her daughters. "Pen, please! Stop it! The girls are home and your yelling isn't going to help."

Penelope stood up and stomped childishly toward the kitchen door. "Maybe not, but, it sure makes me feel a whole lot better!"

"*Penelope*," Renee tried, again.

"Did you hear that, Kris?" Penelope ranted, paying no heed to Renee and oblivious to Paul's wide eyes. "I'm leaving, so that you can have all of the attention, as usual! God forbid I have any, except when I'm telling a joke!"

Paul looked at Renee, his face incredulous. "What's going on?"

"Good bye," Penelope spat as she yanked violently on the door, swinging it wide and letting the cool, Spring air gust through the kitchen.

Paul reached out to catch it, before it slammed shut behind Penelope, and turned, again, to Renee. "Seriously, what the hell is happening?"

Renee didn't make time to answer. Instead, she ran through the kitchen to her front door, just in time to see Penelope rounding the house. She threw open the door and called out, "Pen! Come back!"

Penelope didn't look back. She wrenched open the door of her brand new car - yet another thing she had been thrilled about, her first new car in so many years that she'd lost count. Of course, because of Kris, she couldn't even share that joy. Bloody Kris!

She threw the car into reverse and backed out of the driveway, her pulse throbbing as she made herself mindful to watch for little children and animals. Once on the deserted street, she hit the gas and her tires squealed noisily as she peeled away without a backward glance.

"Wow," Paul said as he watched her disappear from sight. "Who knew Pen had such a temper? Was that the new Eclipse she was driving?"

Renee stood out on her front steps, phone still pressed to her ear and rolled her eyes. Trust Paul to notice the car. "Did you hear that, Kris?" she spoke into the phone. "She is seriously angry. I've never seen her so mad. Ever."

She shook her head and Paul held the door for her as she stepped back inside the house. "We've got to figure out how to fix this. Fast. Or else, things could get really uncomfortable."

Ben was sitting in his home office, doing paperwork, when the door to the garage slammed so hard, it shook the house. He looked up, startled, from his work and called out, "Pen? Is that you?"

He waited for a reply, but, when none came, he got up out of his chair and walked, with tentative steps, down the hallway and toward the kitchen.

"Just when you think you know someone," Penelope was muttering to herself while retrieving a glass from the kitchen cupboard. She turned around to find a Ben, a stunned expression plastered across his face, staring at her as though she was a complete stranger.

"Holy Moses!" Ben exclaimed, at a loss for anything better to say. "Look at you!"

"Well, hell!" Penelope spat. "You, too?"

Ben raised his eyebrows in surprise. "What are you talking about?"

"I'm talking about the issue that everyone is making over my making some changes. God, almighty, you'd think I'd gone and had plastic surgery, or something. Am I supposed to stay exactly the same until I die? It's beyond frustrating!"

"I'm not making an issue, Honey," Ben attempted to clarify. He did not want a repeat of the previous evening. "Not at all. I was just surprised. In fact, I think you look fantastic!"

"As compared to what?"

Ben froze. Crap. He couldn't win and he knew it.

"When I looked frumpy and tired? Frumpy, old Penelope and regular, old Ben. The old married couple before they actually even do the deed!"

Ben's eyes widened in alarmed. She was doing it, again, and he felt as though he was caught in a trap, with no way out. "No, no, I definitely did not say any of that, either."

Penelope, suddenly exhausted, let her shoulders slump. "Okay, fine. I'm sorry. I know that you didn't. I'm just pissed off and worn out. It's been an emotional day and I received a reaction I didn't expect, from the very last person I thought I'd get it from. It's not you."

Ben took a deep breath and nodded, trying valiantly to keep up. It wasn't him. That was good. "Well, for what it's worth, I'm sorry about that. But, really, if it helps, you look stunning, Penelope."

Penelope ducked her head and gave him an appreciative smile. "Thank you."

The phone began to ring and she automatically reached for it. When she heard Renee's voice on the other end, she wished she had left it.

"What," Penelope said, rudely, and placed her glass on the counter top. Ben watched, confused by her sudden change of attitude. "Can't Kris do it? She's the one who's always at the center of everything, isn't she?"

Ben raised an eyebrow, even more perplexed. Penelope loved Kris, what was going on?

"Okay, fine, yes, I'll do it. In fact, I'd love to. More changes for me and more, 'oh, my, goodness, be careful, blah, blah, blah,' for her. What time?"

Ben picked up her glass, poured her water and waited.

"Okay, I'll see you then." Penelope hung up and Ben handed her her water. "Everything okay?" He asked as she drank the glass in one go.

"Yes," she replied, placing the empty glass on the countertop and kicking off her shoes. "Renee was offered a large cake job and she's asked me to help her with the client end of things."

"Doesn't Kris usually do that?"

She cut her eyes at him and Ben shut his mouth. "Yes, she usually does. However, she caught Cameron's cold and can't do it this time. So, I agreed to do it, instead."

Ben nodded and did his best to be non-confrontational. "Well, that's nice of you. I'm sure Renee appreciates it. I don't know why she hasn't hired an actual assistant. Her cake making business --"

"*Divine Designs.*"

"Right, *Divine Designs* is growing by leaps and bounds and she's going to need someone on a full time basis."

I know," Penelope agreed, pushing her hair back from her face and stretching her neck. "I've basically said the same thing to her, but, you know Renee. She takes her time getting to where she needs to be and nothing will force her there."

"Oh, that reminds me," Ben said. "Paul called me, and he and I and Grayson are going to meet up later on, after dinner, for drinks."

Penelope gave him a quizzical look. "Why do I get the feeling it's more than just drinks and idle chitchat?"

"Probably because it was Paul who arranged it." Ben said. "He never initiates us getting together. But, this time he did, so, I'm guessing that there's more going on than he's saying."

Penelope felt a moment of worry. Paul had watched her storm out of his house, not to mention the whole deal with him seeing her with Scott, aka Single Dad. It could end up a nightmare, if Paul decided to say something to Ben. Hopefully, Renee was right and he no longer thought it was anything worth talking about.

"Pen? Is that okay with you?"

"Of course," she said, then smiled as she remembered her new car. Finally, she could share.

"Speaking of fun," she said. "I have something else new, besides my make-over, that I haven't shown yet to anyone. Want to be the first to see it?"

Ben raised an eyebrow, intrigued. "Of course, what is it?"

Penelope reached for his hand and led him to the garage. "Follow me."

Ben walked through the doors of the sports themed bar, aptly named Champs. He paused to let his eyes adjust to the darkened room - taking in the large, wood and brass bar, big screen TVs hanging from the ceilings and the wall of sports themed memorabilia. He didn't know why Paul had chosen such a noisy place to meet, but, such was life.

Grayson, sitting at a pub table with Paul near the back of the room, spotted Ben and raised a hand in greeting. He nodded and threaded his way through the pool tables, and the people milling around them, to arrive at the table.

"Hey, Sport," Grayson teased as Ben unzipped and removed his brown, leather jacket. "Good to see you."

Ben shook his head and grinned. "Sport? Really?" He wrapped his jacket across the back of his chair and sat down.

Grayson snickered and Ben laughed. Sometimes, it seemed that, no matter how old they got, they never stopped being the boys they once were.

"Don't feel too badly," Paul, sitting across the table from Grayson, said, flatly. "I got Skippy."

Ben laughed, again, and ran his fingers through his short, blond hair. "What are you guys having?"

"I've got this one," Grayson replied. "You can get the next round." He waved his hand in the air and a cute, lithe, redhead came over to take their order. She didn't look old enough to be serving drinks.

Ben saw the delighted look on the girl's face when she laid eyes on Grayson. His brother, dressed in dark wash jeans and a dark, purple dress shirt - his dusky blonde hair perfectly messed and his five o-clock shadow groomed to show off his cheek bones - had that effect on women. As long as Ben could remember, women lit up around the man.

"Hey, boys," the waitress flashed them a dimpled smile, cocked her hip to one side and pointed to her name tag, attached above her left breast. "I'm Destiny. What can I start you off with this evening?"

"Hey, Destiny," Grayson smiled, revealing his straight, white teeth. "I'd like to buy a round for my brothers, whatever they want, and we'll start with your super nachos and work our way from there."

Destiny twinkled at Grayson. "Absolutely," she said and reached out a hand to lightly finger the woven fabric of his shirt. "I love this color," she gushed. "Dark purple on men is so cool."

Ben rolled his eyes and exchanged a look with Paul. Were they even in the room?

Paul smiled and nodded at Ben, then cleared his throat. "Eh-hem! I'll have a G & T, Tanqueray, if you have it."

Destiny blinked, pulled her gaze from Grayson and looked at Paul for the first time. In his tan chinos, navy blue golf shirt and sensibly cut hair, the two men couldn't have been more opposite.

Destiny recovered her poise and plastered on a bright smile. "Of course, Sweetie! Whatever you want, I'll find it."

"Thanks --" Paul began, but, she had already lost interest.

"And, you?" She addressed Ben.

"I'll have the same," he replied. No need to confuse the girl, when she was clearly befuddled by Grayson.

Destiny winked and returned her attention to Grayson. "I don't think I got your order, what strikes *your* fancy?"

Ben swallowed and looked away. The emphasis she put on 'your' was almost enough to send him over the edge into laughter. He kept his eyes on the table, pretending to be interested in the coasters, until Grayson had ordered his scotch and the girl left.

"Jeez," Paul exhaled.

"I know," Ben agreed.

"What?" Grayson asked.

"Oh, come on," Paul said, raising an eyebrow at Grayson. "Like you don't know."

Grayson looked at him, confused, and then turned to Ben. "Am I missing something here?"

Ben laughed. "No. Just the usual. A woman practically tap dances in front of you for your attention and you don't even register she's doing it."

Grayson frowned. "What? Her? Destiny? She was just being nice, doing her job."

Paul let out a bark of laughter.

"You guys," Grayson said, shaking his head. "Always giving the worst motives --"

"Fine," Ben placated. "Moving on?"

"Fine by me," Grayson said, leaning back in his chair.

"Excellent," Ben replied, ignoring Grayson's weakly veiled accusation that he and Paul were the ones with the problem. He turned to Paul. "So, what's up?"

Paul settled back in his seat. "Nothing, really. Why do you ask?"

"You called this meeting."

"It was Renee's idea, actually."

"Renee?" Grayson asked.

"Yeah," Paul nodded. "She said she thought it had been too long since we've had a guy's night out."

"Wow," Grayson said, impressed. "Good wife."

"You betchya."

"How's Cam?" Ben asked.

"Better, much better. Except," Grayson shook his head. "Now, of course, Kris has it."

"Yeah, I heard," Ben said, and then wished he'd kept his mouth shut when Grayson raised an eyebrow.

"Really? I'm surprised that your fiancée is saying anything at all about Kris right now."

Paul sat up straighter. After Penelope had stormed out of his house, Renee had filled him in about the big blow up between the two women.

"What's going on there, anyway?" Ben questioned.

Grayson paused as Destiny arrived to put their drinks on the table. "I'll be right back with your nachos," she said, fluttering her eyelashes at Grayson.

"Thank you," Grayson smiled politely.

Paul watched her sashay away and rolled his eyes at Ben.

"What do you mean?" Grayson leaned forward and picked up where they'd left off. "Pen hasn't told you anything?"

Ben shook his head and picked up his glass. "No, not really. I know that there was an altercation of some kind, but, otherwise, she's not saying too much and keeping things to herself."

Paul cleared his throat and the two men looked at him expectantly. "Let me tell it, okay? I think I've got the clearest picture about it. I was there, sort of, at the end, and the rest I got from Renee."

Ben listened to the story, the waitress came and went with their food, Grayson didn't inadvertently flirt with her and, finally, he couldn't keep his thoughts to himself. "I've got a bad feeling," he said, massaging his forehead to ease the tension in his skull.

Paul dipped a red nacho chip into guacamole and looked at him quizzically. "About what? I'm sure that they'll get it sorted out in a few days. These things never last."

"No, not about that. Well, not directly, anyway." Ben fiddled with his coaster. "I'm worried about Pen. She's been acting strangely. Way out of character. That temper you described at your place? That's new. Not her usual state of mind."

"So, she's showing a bit of temper, what's the worry? You should see the way that Kris gets when I've pissed her off." Grayson commented.

"If it was just her temper," Ben acknowledged. "That would be one thing, but, it's not. She seems angry, or frustrated, or something. I've been having a hard time keeping up."

"Maybe it's work," Paul offered.

"No, I don't think so," Ben shook his head.

"Have you asked her?" Grayson said.

"I haven't had the chance! She's been so prickly, I've been afraid to open my mouth." He swallowed the last of his drink and set the glass down on the table. "Now, she's suddenly making changes ... And, they're big changes, not just little ones."

His brothers stared at him, mute, and Ben threw down his trump card. "She bought a new car!"

"I saw it!" Paul pointed at Ben. "The Eclipse, right? That was Penelope's car? Seriously?"

"Oh, yeah, it's brand, spanking new, all right. Red and sporty, a coupe for Christ's sake!"

"Wow," Grayson said, his voice full of admiration. "Those are good looking cars. Good for Pen."

"No!" Ben shook his head, annoyed that he wasn't being understood. "Not good. You're completely missing the point."

"Okay," Grayson said, as he reached for a nacho chip. "Enlighten us."

"It's like this. On the surface, it might appear that what she's done is a 'good for Pen' sort of thing. But, I'm thinking it might be just the opposite. More like a, 'bad for Pen and Ben', sort of thing."

"How do you figure?" Grayson looked confused.

"I get it," Paul offered and turned to Grayson. "Ben's worried that the car is an indicator of bigger things not spoken. Am I right?"

"You are exactly right!" Ben nodded enthusiastically, extending his hand to high-five his brother. Grayson rolled his eyes and looked a little put off by the insightful, talk show moment.

"And," Ben elaborated. "It's not just the car, either. She had a whole new makeover. You should see her. Huge change. Although," he acknowledged, with a tilt of his head toward Paul. "I guess you've already seen her."

Paul nodded and picked up his drink. He wasn't about to comment on how fantastic she had looked. He was a lot smarter than that.

Ben leaned his elbows on the table. "Anyway, just like the car, it isn't so much the actual makeover that's the issue. It's how she *is*, inside of that makeover, that I'm concerned about."

"What are you saying," Grayson asked, skeptically. "What's the bottom line? You think Pen's cheating, or something?"

"No!" Ben looked appalled at the suggestion. "No, I don't think *that*. But, for the record, she did make a comment about us being an old married couple --"

Grayson snorted and Paul frowned at him.

"It's not funny, man," Ben insisted.

Grayson held up a hand. "No, sorry, I know that technically it isn't. But, technicalities aside --"

"What? What are you saying? You think we act like we're an old married couple?"

"No, not exactly, but, you have to admit, you guys are really into your routines."

"Oh, whatever," Ben scoffed. "And you and Kris aren't like that?"

"No, of course we are, but," Grayson reasoned. "We have three kids and have actually been married for a while."

"Holy shit," Ben said, realization hitting him like a brick. "She's going to leave me."

"No," Paul stated. "Now you're just being stupid." He glared at Grayson, resisting the urge to belt him.

Grayson held up his hands in a 'what did I do?' gesture.

"Am I?" Ben said, dropping his head into his hands and speaking toward the table top.

"Of course you are," Paul affirmed. "There's no way --"

"'Cause, I don't think so," Ben pulled his hands from his head and sat up straight. Paul thought he looked a bit wild-eyed.

"I have to do something. Something big to get her attention. Otherwise, she might start rethinking everything. Us. Our engagement. Everything."

Paul felt terrible. He wished he could do something to reassure his brother. He had been thinking, on his drive over, of mentioning that he had seen Penelope with that slick dude at the school, but, now, he shelved that idea. He didn't want to add more stress to Ben's, already overwrought, mind.

"Oh, *come on*, Ben," Grayson piped up, trying to infuse some rational into the situation. "It's Pen we're talking about, here. There's no way that she's leaving you."

"You don't know that for sure." Ben said, leaning back in his chair and folding his arms across his chest.

"Okay, fine," Grayson relented. "Fair enough, I don't."

Paul shot him an incredulous look and Grayson quickly amended. "But, I do know Pen and I honestly think that she'd talk to you, try to sort things out with you, before she'd just chuck it all."

Ben reluctantly nodded and Paul grinned encouragingly. "You see? You know it, too. No matter what, chucking it is not Penelope's style."

Grayson quickly backed Paul up. "He's right, Ben. We're both right. Old married couple teasing aside, Penelope's way too much in love with you, not to mention level headed, for that."

Ben reflected upon the recent actions of his fiancée, storming out over one simple comment; the sudden make over and new car; the comments about them being an old married couple, and he wondered. Maybe, she had decided that being level headed wasn't working for her anymore and it was time to try something new? He couldn't bring himself to air those thoughts, he needed more time to think.

"Maybe you're right," he conceded.

"Of course we are," Grayson insisted, hugely relieved that the awkward moment was being shelved. He patted Ben on the shoulder. "She's probably just needs a few changes because her life has gotten too routine. Women can be that way."

Ben looked at his brother quizzically. "You sound awfully certain about that," he said. "Everything okay with you?"

Grayson looked guilty, then guarded. "Me? Yeah, everything is fine. Why do you ask?"

"No particular reason. Other than that fact that you looked pretty knowing, when you mentioned a woman needing changes." Ben raised his hands, noncommittally. "But, hey, what do I know?"

Paul took a sip of his drink and kept quiet. Renee had told him about Kris' laments, too. If Grayson wasn't offering it up to talk about, he sure as heck wasn't going to be the one to get that ball rolling.

Grayson shrugged. Something he didn't do often. The movement looked almost unnatural on him. "It's nothing, just Kris. I'm not even too sure what it is, to be honest. I just know that she's been feeling out of sorts lately. Sounds a bit like Pen, to tell you the truth. She hasn't gone and bought a new *car* or anything," he paused and flashed a grin at Ben.

Ben shook his head and laughed.

"Holy crap, are we ever a bunch of downers," Paul said. It was time to brighten the mood. "The Miller brothers of old we are not! Once upon a time, we were the life of the party and, now, all we can do is whine about are our women and their grievances."

Ben and Grayson both smiled and then started laughing. Paul was right, they did sound like a bunch of sniffling kids.

Paul pointed at Ben. "Buy me another drink and let's play some darts, or pool, or *something* that doesn't involve whining, and leave our women crap at the door."

"You're on," Ben said and waved Destiny over. She grinned at them as she sauntered across the room, her hips swinging.

"So, boys, looks like you're making it a party. Can I interest you in some La Bandera Mexicana shots? They're two for one tonight."

Grayson grinned, appreciatively, and Destiny visibly caught her breath. He didn't notice. "I think we'll definitely have a piece of that action," he nodded. "We'll start with two apiece."

He pointed a finger at his brothers. "I'm buying, so shut up and drink."

"Done." Paul replied, and Ben nodded briskly, keeping his mouth firmly shut. There was a time to talk and there was a time to drink and hang with your brothers. He knew the difference.

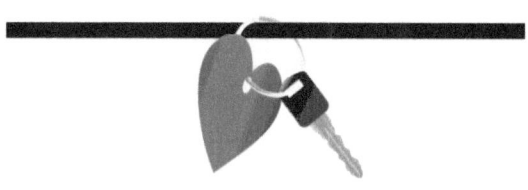

Four

Penelope parked beside the curb of Renee's house, honked the car horn and grinned. She still couldn't believe that she'd brazenly walked into the Mitsubishi dealership and traded her old, stable, gray station wagon for this fiery red, sports car. It was so out of character, her old character, and she felt like a teenager every time she got behind the wheel.

"This is such a great car!" Renee exclaimed as she opened the door and slipped into the passenger seat beside Penelope.

"I know!" Penelope said, gleefully. "I'm still in shock that I bought it!"

"You look right at home in it, too," Renee said, grinning approvingly at Penelope. "Look at you! So hip and put together!"

Penelope blushed. She had been really pleased with herself when she got ready that morning.

"I love those jeans and your blouse, wow. That green is gorgeous on you." Renee leaned in to peer at Penelope's feet in the foot well. "Oh! I love those shoes! The butterflies, I could never pull those off. God, I feel like a slob next to you."

"Stop!" Penelope slapped playfully at Renee's arm.

"It's true," Renee insisted, pointing at her outfit.

"Oh, please," Penelope rolled her eyes. Renee was anything, but slovenly. In her red silk, knee length, flower print dress; pared with a navy blue, crushed velvet jacket that made her blue eyes pop, and finished with knee high, brown leather boots, she looked as she always did - chic and hip, with a touch of Bohemian flare.

"Just stating facts," Renee said. "You look sharp. Don't up the bar if you aren't prepared for the feedback, Missy."

"Okay, okay," Penelope laughed. "Thank you. Can we go back to how great the car is, now?"

"It has everything," Renee said, seamlessly switching topics. She peered at the dashboard, checking out all of the switches and whatnots. "All the bells and whistles."

"I know, all it needs is an automatic coffee dispenser," Penelope joked.

"Speaking of which," Renee said. "Did you have any coffee yet this morning? Do you want to make a stop? My treat."

"Absolutely," Penelope agreed as she pulled the car away from the curb. "I tiptoed out of the house. Ben was dead to the world. I think he and the other two really tied one on last night."

Renee snickered. "I know. When Paul came in, he started singing love songs and I had to do some major work to shut him up so he wouldn't wake the girls."

Penelope laughed, appreciatively, but kept mum about Ben's drunken babbling about whether or not an old married guy could do *this*, and then had dropped to the floor in an attempt to do push -ups. Not pretty. He'd ended up falling asleep, dead to the world, on the kitchen floor and Penelope had had no choice but to leave him and cover him with a blanket. Sometime, during the night, he'd managed to crawl onto the couch in the family room and that was where he was, when she'd left the house.

"So," she changed the subject. "Where are we headed?"

Renee pulled her iPhone from her bag. "It's an architectural firm, if you can believe it."

"They're open Saturdays?"

"I don't think so," Renee replied. "But, they have someone there to meet us. I was told that they want to keep things relatively under wraps, because the cakes are for a surprise party. I'm going to be making individual, personalized cakes for every person invited to the party."

"Wow, seriously?" Penelope said, impressed. "That could be a whole lot of cakes."

"Tell me about it," Renee nodded. "I haven't been given final numbers, yet. We'll get that today."

"Cute bag, by the way."

"Thanks," Renee said and touched her leather satchel. "It's perfect for this sort of thing. Professional enough to make me look like I know what I'm doing and practical enough to store all of my stuff."

"Renee," Penelope said as she pulled the car into line at the coffee shop drive-thru. "Why aren't you hiring an assistant? You need one. I don't get why you haven't."

Renee waited a beat, as Penelope ordered their coffees.

"Because," she replied, when Penelope was finished. "I haven't had the time. Not to mention, not just anyone will do."

Penelope received their coffees and handed one to Renee. The other, she set into one of the cup holders between their seats. "None of that's true, and you know it."

Renee was about to protest, but, Penelope shook her head. "Hear me out. You *do* have someone who's perfect for the job and, even though I'm extremely pissed right off at her right now, I still know that she's perfect."

Renee set her coffee cup into the second holder. "You really don't need to be so mad at Kris. It was all a big misunderstanding and, even though I know you don't want to hear it, she didn't mean to offend you and she's really sorry."

Penelope stiffened in her seat as she pulled out of the parking lot and back onto the road. "Is it here we turn?" She gestured to her left, avoiding all eye contact with Renee.

"Pen?" Renee said, gently. "You do know that Kris loves you, right? And, if she came across as less than that, it was only because she's going through some stuff right now, too."

Penelope snorted, derisively. "Please! Is Ms. Perfect of the mind that she has troubles? What troubles are they? She can't decide how she wants to style her gorgeous hair? Which expensive outfit to wear?"

"Okay, that's enough!" Renee exploded. She had had it. "You need to pull your head out of your ass, or get your issues bagged up, or *something* like that and get things straightened out!"

"But --"

"No! No buts!" Renee slapped her knee for emphasis. "You are acting childish, you're too damned old for it and, if you don't stop, I'm going to send you to either Zoe's or Alexa's room for a time out!"

Penelope sniggered and bit her lip. The very idea of being sent to one of Renee's daughter's rooms was hysterical.

"Okay, then," Renee said, matter of fact. "Are you ready to hear something, besides your own childish voice?"

Penelope glanced out of the corner of her eye at Renee and snickered, again. "Yes, *Mom*, I'm ready. Go ahead."

Renee exhaled in relief and picked up her coffee. "Thank goodness! I was starting to worry."

"Oh, please, you know I would have eventually gotten over it and come around."

"Perhaps," Renee said. "But, I don't think you really get what's going on with Kris, right now. Otherwise, I don't think you would have become so angry, in the first place."

Penelope nodded and turned into the parking lot of the architectural firm. She swung her car into a space and cut the engine. "We're here."

"Okay, quickly, before we go in," Renee lifted Penelope's coffee from its holder and handed it to her to keep her quiet. "The reader's digest version is, Kris is feeling like her life isn't about her, anymore. She's become all about the boys and Grayson, keeping the house and all of that, and is feeling really scared that anything she had of her own, is long gone."

"That's crazy --"

"Yes, I know that and you know that, but, she is seriously fretting. She thinks that, by the time she'll need her own back, it will be so far gone, she'll be sunk."

Penelope sipped her coffee, then shook her head. "Not likely."

"Exactly, but, Kris needs to prove it to herself, that those kind of worries are crazy, before she'll let them go. Make sense?"

Penelope nodded.

"And, by the way, in regards to your comment, yes, I absolutely am aware that Kris is perfect for the job of my assistant. But, I've been treading carefully, because I think if I offer it too soon, she'll see it as a pity offer and turn me down. Then, I'll really be in trouble. I can't even think about that."

"So, what are you going to do?"

Renee exhaled, then smiled. "I'll continue to do it this way for a bit longer and when I feel the time is right, I'll offer it to her." She swung open her door. "Okay, for now, we're done. We need to get inside, act professional and get a handle on what this job is all about. Seize the day."

Penelope nodded and stepped out of the car. She smiled to herself, amused that there was no way she could ever lock her keys in her car now. Granted, if she hadn't locked them into the old car, she wouldn't have met Scott. And, not meeting Scott could have meant that she didn't have the impetus to actually make the changes she had been wanting to make ... And, no changes would have meant the same old life ...

"Pen?" Renee said. "You coming?"

Penelope pressed the lock function on her key chain. "Coming," she nodded. It was time to look forward. It was time for coffee and cake.

"Wow, quite the place," Renee commented, in hushed tones. She and Penelope had been led into a conference room, by a scarily efficient looking receptionist, and were awaiting their contact person.

Penelope nodded. "I know, look at the window treatments, for goodness sake." She pointed at the curtains, their pattern clearly Asian inspired with rich colors and glinting gold. "Do you think they're genuine silk?"

Renee shrugged. "You've got me," she said as she took in the long, wooden conference table, polished and gleaming under the recessed lighting, and adorned by cushy, tall backed chairs. "But, looking at the rest of this place. It wouldn't exactly surprise me."

Penelope smiled and pointed to the side of the wide room. "Check out the silver coffee service on the hutch."

"Any minute now, I'm going to start tip-toeing like Alexa and Zoe," Renee joked and mimed taking exaggerated steps.

"Hello!" A deep male voice interrupted their conversation and Renee stumbled into Penelope in her surprise, nearly knocking them both to the floor.

"Oh!" Renee said, as she pulled herself upright. "I'm so sorry," she began and then stopped when she realized that she didn't need to bother apologizing. The man, who was seriously gorgeous, wasn't even looking at her.

Penelope, on the other hand, was slack-jawed as she stared full on at the man.

"You!" The, seriously gorgeous, man said.

Renee swung her head back and forth from Penelope, to the man, then back, again. "Am I missing something, here?"

"What are the odds?" The man asked and started to laugh.

"Okay, seriously. Please, someone fill me in."

Penelope managed to close her mouth and turned to Renee. "Sorry," she said, her voice strained and formal. "Renee, this is Scott."

"Oh!" Renee blurted, and then tried to look less startled and, instead, more pleasantly interested. "I mean, *oh*, and how do you know each other? That is, I'm assuming, from the way that you are acting, that you know each other?"

Penelope rolled her eyes. Smooth. "Yes, I think I mentioned that Scott was the kind person who helped me out with my car, when I locked my keys inside?"

"Yes! That's right!" Renee enthused, a little too over the top and, quite frankly, slightly too British. Penelope wouldn't have been surprised if her next words were, 'Jolly Good!'

"That's why his name sounded familiar when he was given as my contact!" Renee said to Penelope. She turned to Scott, as though he hadn't already heard her. "That's why your name sounded familiar."

Penelope resisted the urge to groan. Renee was being about as cool as a jalapeno pepper. She wouldn't have blamed Scott if he was under the impression that, since they had met, she'd never shut up about him.

"Right, of course," Scott said, an amused glint in his eye. "Makes sense. And, I'm going to take a leap and assume you're *Divine Designs*, correct?"

Renee nodded and kept her mouth shut. She didn't want to risk anymore babbling. It was better to let the man talk and just listen.

"Well, thanks for coming on such short notice. I know that the boss was seriously impressed by your willingness to be so accommodating. I've got some papers here outlining what he wants done."

"So, this is your firm?" Penelope looked around the room with renewed interest.

"Well, not *mine*, per se --"

"No, no, I just meant --"

Renee watched them banter. It bordered upon painful. "Those papers?" She interrupted, trying to move things along.

"Right!" Scott handed over a hefty stack of papers, his eyes drifting back to Penelope's face. "I'm sorry, I don't mean to be forward, but, I just have to say, you look so different than when I last saw you --"

"Oh, right," Penelope chuckled, inordinately pleased that he'd noticed. "I decided it was time for a change. I guess you could say that I was done with the background phase of my life, you know? So, I decided to kick things up a notch." She tapered off, noting that she was babbling. Something about the man just made her want to babble.

"I don't know anything about background," he said. "Because, obviously, I definitely noticed you the first time we met. But, this change," he gestured with his hand, moving it up and down. "It just makes you noticeable, in a different sort way."

Penelope felt herself begin to flush. Scott was contemplating her in such a speculative manner, she couldn't remember the last time she'd been gazed at so attentively. If she was to be honest with herself, she'd say, she liked it.

"Never mind me," she recovered, pointing at him. Gone were the casual track pants and t-shirt. He was gorgeous in black, tailored, dress pants and an open collared, black and white, pinstriped dress shirt. "You clean up, yourself."

Scott had the good grace to look flattered

"Okaaay," Renee said, trying, for a second time, to move things along. "Well, Scott, it was wonderful meeting you. And, after I read everything, we should be in touch with whom, exactly?"

"Me," he confirmed, pulling his broad shoulders back and standing a bit straighter. "Definitely, me."

"Fine," Renee began, and then wondered why she'd bothered. His attention was all for Penelope.

Scott turned to Penelope. "I don't recall you mentioning in our last conversation that you did creative baking --"

"No! No, I don't." Penelope giggled. "No, I'm just an accountant."

"Right," Renee tried, again. Nothing. She wondered if she should just pull out one of the cushy chairs at the conference table and make herself at home.

Penelope placed a hand on her hip, cocked her head thoughtfully to one side and twirled a piece of her hair around her finger as she gazed at Scott. "I seem to keep on doing that, don't I?"

"What's that?" He asked, a small smile playing at his lips as he watched her.

"Saying that I don't have something, or don't do something, when it actually appears the opposite. First it was the kids, who were my nephews, and, now, it's the baking ..."

"Yeah," Scott agreed, kicking his smile into full gear. "You do. So, what's the lowdown this time, *Penelope*?"

Penelope caught her breath and sobered up quickly, when he said her name. "I'm just assisting," she said, daring to meet his eye, straight on.

"Me," Renee added, trying to get a foothold in the conversation. "She's assisting me."

"As I said, I'm an accountant. But, my schedule is flexible and Renee," Penelope gestured to Renee, while she resisted the desire to wave madly. "Needed someone, a lowly assistant, to make sure all the details are attended to, so that she can work her creative magic unfettered."

It was Renee's turn to allow her jaw to drop. Penelope was practically gushing with praise about her work. She had no idea she held her in such high regard.

"Well, while I know that Renee's creativity is without question," Scott returned Penelope's steady gaze. "I highly doubt that your help is in any way *lowly*."

Okay, thought Renee, gushing praise aside, enough was enough. "How right you are, Scott!" She blurted.

It worked, Scott actually gave her his attention.

"Penelope is one of the most organized people I know. Ask any of her clients. Not that you'll need to, as you'll get to find that out first hand, working closely with her on the details."

"Really?" Scott's face broke into a pleased smile as he shifted his focus back to Penelope. "You'll be my contact person?"

Oh crap, Renee thought. That was not the best thing to say to move things along. "Yup! Penelope will be your woman," she winced, not daring to make eye contact with Penelope, and bulldozed forward. "So, you have my card, if you need anything. Just call and Penelope can get it handled."

Penelope nodded along with everything Renee was saying. She was afraid she might say something horrifyingly teenaged like, "You have nice eyes", if she opened her mouth again. Staying silent seemed her best option.

"Okay, well, we must run," Renee tugged on Penelope's arm.

"Right," Scott nodded and extended his hand.

Renee remembered her manners and paused to shake his hand. She looked up to meet his warm, hazel eyes and thought that, were she not happily married, she could see how she might desire to slip in there. Poor Penelope. For that matter, poor Ben.

Scott extended his hand for a second time, to Penelope. Their eyes met and held for a fraction longer than necessary.

Renee nudged Penelope and cleared her throat. "Okay, well, again, thanks so much! We'll leave you to the rest of your day. Looking forward to a great partnership."

"Us, too," Scott replied, as the two women slipped out the door, Renee leading Penelope firmly by the arm, and the door shut softly behind them.

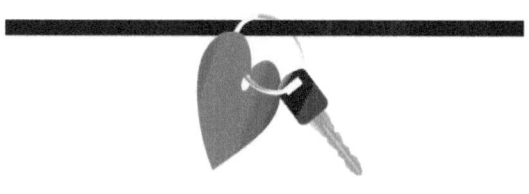

FIVE

"Hey, Pen," Grayson's voice held a tremor of uncertainty as he spoke into the phone.

Penelope cleared her throat, determined to be as non-threatening as possible. "Hey, Gray, what's up?"

Grayson exhaled, relieved that Penelope sounded pleasant. "Well, I wouldn't ask if I didn't have to, but, Kris is still sick --"

"Right, you need the boys taken to school. No problem."

It was Monday morning and Penelope had taken the remainder of the weekend to think about what Renee had told her about Kris. She didn't want to be angry and, upon reflection, she didn't think it was worth bad feelings. She was ready to put the issue behind her.

"I can be over in about a half hour," she told Grayson, while she glanced at her closet, deciding which new clothes that she would wear. "Is that okay?"

"That's more than okay, that's perfect," Grayson enthused. "You're a life saver. Thanks, so much, Pen."

"Don't worry about it, I'm glad to do it." Penelope tightened the sash on her robe and sat down on her bed. "Before we go, can you do me a favor?"

"Anything."

"Tell Kris that I've been thinking for the past couple of days and I'm not angry with her, anymore."

Grayson smiled. He knew that it would get worked out. "Got it."

"Tell her I'll talk to her later, when she's feeling better."

"Okay," Grayson replied, pleased. Kris needed Penelope, her best friend, in her corner. "I'll tell her."

"Thanks," Penelope said. "And, also, Gray? I don't think Kris has picked up on it, but, she could really be a valuable asset to Renee."

Grayson furrowed his brow and leaned against his kitchen counter top. "I don't follow."

"Well, I don't want to step on any toes, or anything, but, if Kris was encouraged to see it, she would realize that not only is Renee in desperate need of a full time assistant, but, she would be the perfect person to take on that role."

Grayson inhaled sharply. Of course, it was so obvious. He should have seen it. "You know, Pen, I think you're on to something, here. Does Renee think the same way?"

"Oh, definitely."

"Why hasn't she said?"

"She doesn't want to push Kris before she's ready." Penelope walked across the room to her dresser and started rummaging through her drawer. "She says she wants to let it fall naturally into place, but, I think," Penelope pulled out her new red bra, with a satisfied smile. "Some things need to be encouraged to fall *naturally* into place, you know?"

Grayson laughed. "Absolutely. I completely agree. Okay, I'll do what I can to set the idea into motion --"

"Carefully, though." Penelope cautioned. "We don't want either of them to think we're forcing the issue."

"Got it. Tread carefully."

"Excellent. I'll see you in a bit to pick up the boys."

"Right," Grayson nodded. "Thanks, again."

"Remember to tell Kris that I'm not mad anymore."

"I will. See you."

Penelope hung up the phone, pleased. You see, she thought, as she loosened her robe and let it drop to the bedroom floor. Change can be good.

"Okay, girls, got your backpacks?" Paul opened his back door, ready to usher the twins into his Escalade.

"Getting it!" Zoe replied, full of zest.

"Oh, no, Poppy," Paul looked down at their pint sized Yorkie, jumping up at the pant legs of his suit. "You stay with Mommy."

"My lunch, I need my lunch!" Zoe exclaimed, full of purpose.

"Got mine!" Alexa shouted as she pushed by Zoe and ran down the front path toward Paul's SUV.

"Your lunch is in your backpack, I think," Paul told Zoe, as he watched Alexa heave open the vehicle's black door and then disappear from sight. He turned to Renee. "Right, Mommy?"

Renee cut her eyes at him. "Yes, of course it is. I always put them in the backpacks, don't I? Why would today be any different?"

"Okay, then," Paul made quick work of maneuvering Zoe outside, while blocking the dog from following along. "You heard Mommy. You're all set."

Zoe, satisfied that everything was in order, skipped down the path toward the waiting vehicle. Paul turned back to Renee. "Everything all right?" He asked.

Renee looked at him, her arms folded tightly across her torso. "Oh, sure, fine. I just don't particularly enjoy you undermining me in front of my daughters!"

Paul's eyes widened. "Undermining you?"

Renee rolled her eyes and then reached to pick up Poppy, before she managed to squeeze by Paul. "Oh, whatever, Paul. Granted, the girls are too young to notice, but, I'm aware of what you're doing."

"What I'm doing?" He frowned and shook his head. "Well, then, you need to tell me what that is, because even I don't know."

Renee narrowed her eyes and tucked Poppy under her arm. "The whole passive-aggressive thing of helping out, and then questioning if I'm doing what I usually do. As though my work commitments are getting so big, that I can't even remember the simple task of making sure that the girl's lunches are in their bags!"

"Okay," Paul said, trying to keep the bewilderment out of his voice as he attempted to pat things down. "Hon, I don't know where this is coming from, but, I do think we need to talk this out further. Unfortunately, we can't right now because I have about two minutes grace and then the girls will be late and I'll have to write them a note --"

"You see? There it is! I can write a late note, Paul! Even though I'm so busy with my clients right now that I'm feeling pulled in every different direction, it doesn't mean I cannot write two lousy late notes!"

Paul knew when he was beaten. He cleared his throat. "Of course not. I know that you can. But, please, can we discuss this later? Please?"

Renee exhaled and waved her free hand at him. "Yes, fine. Just go. We'll talk about it later."

Paul closed the door, straightened his shoulders and shot his cuffs. Where in the hell did that come from, he thought, as he sprinted to his vehicle. First Penelope goes off the deep end and, now, it seemed it was Renee's turn. He prayed it would somehow resolve itself, before he returned home at the end of the day.

"Ready to go, girls?" He said, keeping his voice cheerful as he slipped behind the wheel and stuck his key into the ignition. "All buckled in?"

"Yes!" The twins said in unison.

"But, we have to hurry today, Daddy," Zoe added. "Amanda, in my class, is bringing her new hamster to show us and I don't want to miss it."

Paul nodded and gave silent thanks that, at least for now, they were still little girls, with little girl problems. When they got to be teenagers, all bets were off.

"Okay, got your jackets, your backpacks, lunches?" Penelope pulled open the car door and Kyle, Kevin and Cameron tumbled out of the backseat.

"Got it!" Kyle answered, as he helped Kevin with his bag.

"Okay, we only have a moment to spare," Penelope reported. "Kyle, Kevin, eyes on me."

The two boys stopped their fidgeting and looked up at their Aunt.

"Remember, you're looking for me, not your Mom, after school. Right?"

The boys nodded, in unison.

She spoke directly to Kyle, as she reached for Cameron's hand. "You'll make sure that Kevin gets to his classroom, right, K?"

"Yes, Auntie Pen," he grinned.

Penelope thought that he was going to be like his father, charming, handsome and trouble. At least until he met the right girl to keep him in line.

"Thank you," she smiled back at him, and then watched as the two boys waved and disappeared around the side of the school.

"Wow, a third one, today, huh?"

Penelope felt a shiver run up her spine when she heard the deep voice behind her. She spun on her kitten heel, pulling Cameron along with her, and couldn't stop the huge grin from enveloping her face when she locked eyes with Scott.

"Scott," she said, trying to keep her voice casual. He was dressed, again, in his black track pants and runners, topped off with a green shirt that did wonders for his hazel eyes. "How are you?"

"I'm good," he smiled, flicking his eyes downward to the deep cleavage at the opening of her red blouse, then back to her face. "Actually, now, I'm great."

Penelope's breath caught in her throat. She had spent extra time on her hair and make-up, as well as wearing her best bra for confidence, and it was turning out to be completely worth the effort.

"So, not the Volvo today, huh?" He appraised her new car as he spoke and Penelope found herself hoping he approved.

"No," Penelope replied. "After the fiasco with my keys, I figured it was time for a change."

"Quite the change," he offered, and smiled intimately at her. "It suits you."

"Thanks," Penelope managed to stammer, breathing deeply to keep her cool.

"So," Scott asked. "We haven't been introduced, who's your companion?"

Penelope followed his gaze and looked down at Cameron, still firmly holding her hand. He was appraising Scott, with a watchful expression that only a four year old could create.

"This," she said. "Is Cameron. He's my --" she stammered, hesitant to make reference, no matter how indirect, to her almost married life. "Well, he's Kyle and Kevin's younger brother."

Scott grinned at Cameron. Cameron did not return the smile.

Penelope gave Cameron's hand a gentle squeeze. "Isn't that right?"

Cameron nodded, still giving Scott a steady stare.

"Do you want to say, 'hello', Cam?" Penelope ventured.

"Hello," Cameron said, levelly.

"Cameron," Scott extended his hand, doing his best not to chuckle. He dropped his smile and matched Cameron's serious demeanor. "Nice to meet you."

Cameron hesitated for a fraction of a second, released Penelope's hand to shake Scott's, and then thrust it back into Penelope's grasp.

"Nice job," Penelope praised.

Cameron rewarded her with a small smile, before returning his gaze to stare stoically at Scott.

"So, anyway," Scott said, his voice low, warm and inviting. "I'm really glad I ran into you."

Penelope stood a little straighter, her blue-green eyes bright. "Really? Why's that?"

"I was wondering if you might have some time free, soon, to go for coffee."

Penelope blinked, taken off guard. Somehow, in her fantasy of seeing him again, nowhere in there had she imagined he'd ask her out.

"What I mean is," he clarified. "I have some stuff that needs to be discussed, in regards to the cake project, and I figured that it might be more pleasant to do so in person. Maybe meet for coffee ..."

"Oh," Penelope nodded. "Of course, that makes sense."

Scott kept his eyes on her full lips as she talked and Penelope resisted the urge to lick them with her tongue. She didn't want to send that message!

"So, um," she cleared her throat and hoped she wouldn't squeak. "That sounds really good. Really good. And, smart, too."

"Auntie Pen is my *Auntie*, you know," Cameron suddenly spoke up, looking directly at Scott. "And, Uncle Ben? He isn't just my Daddy's brother. He's my *Uncle*, too. Auntie Penelope and Uncle Ben."

Subtle as a sledge hammer, Penelope thought, as the beginning of an embarrassed flush heated her exposed throat.

Scott looked at Cameron and smiled. "That makes perfect sense, buddy."

Cameron nodded.

"So, umm, did you have a day in mind?" Penelope shifted from one foot to the next.

"I'm available today, but, if that's no good, then, pretty much every day, at some point, I'm free. Just let me know what your schedule is like."

"Today would be wonderful!" Penelope winced at her enthusiasm and tried to look chipper, as opposed to needy. "First, of course, I have to get this young man to preschool, but, then, my schedule is flexible."

Scott beamed. "Perfect! I have time after lunch, today, so ..."

"Why don't I give you my card." Penelope pulled gently on her hand, still locked in Cameron's grasp. It didn't budge. She tugged, again. Nothing. The boy had a death grip on her hand.

"Having a little trouble, there?" Scott chuckled.

"Oh, uh," Penelope stammered, surprised at Cameron. "Just need to get my hand back."

Cameron looked straight ahead, as though he wasn't a part of anything that was happening.

"Cam? Buddy?" Penelope jiggled their joined hands and queried him. "Auntie needs her hand back for a moment, okay?"

Cameron nodded, then acquiesced, slowly releasing his grip on Penelope's hand. She flexed her freed fingers and grinned at Scott. "Whew," she said, trying to bypass the awkward moment as she turned her attention to rummaging in her bag.

"Quite the grip, there," Scott offered, an amused smirk still on his face.

"Here it is." Penelope thrust her business card at Scott. "My cell number is on there, so, when you know you're free, call me and we can meet."

Cameron reached out and reclaimed Penelope's hand. Oh, boy.

Scott nodded and tucked her card into the pocket of his track pants. "Done. I'll let you go and get Cameron off to school and I'll call you around lunch time to set it up."

He grinned, again, at Cameron. "See you around, Buddy. Make sure you let your Auntie have that hand back, to drive, and have a good day at school."

Penelope laughed. "See you later," she said, and watched as he jogged away. Nice rear view.

"Okay, you," she said, giving Cameron her full attention, all business. He was watching her, as carefully as he had been observing Scott. "Time to get you into your school."

Cameron walked beside her and waited as she pulled open the door to her new car. He released her hand, hopped into the back, tucked his sturdy, little body into his car seat and, as Penelope buckled him in, offered his sage observation.

"That man isn't like Uncle Ben, is he Auntie Penelope? He's *nothing* like Uncle Ben."

Penelope sat in her parked car and concentrated upon her breathing. When Scott had called her, barely an hour after seeing her at the school, to invite her out for coffee, she had been surprised. While she had hoped he would follow through with his suggestion that they meet, she hadn't expected he'd be so speedy about it.

That's neither here, nor there, she told herself. He has business to discuss, why shouldn't he be efficient about arranging for them to get together?

Her logical side wasn't having it. You shouldn't be here, it was telling her. Especially all dressed up in heels and a low cut blouse. Do the smart thing, leave this parking lot, call the man back and arrange to meet him at his office, in his boardroom, with witnesses.

Penelope ignored her logical side and stepped out of her car. She smoothed her new, black linen trousers, pleased at the way that they flattered her backside and smoothed out her slightly rounded stomach.

It's fine, she told herself. They were going to be out in public, at a coffee shop of all places, discussing business. Get a grip. It wasn't like she was running off to a hotel room to meet the guy. It was all above board.

Penelope glanced at the cars parked around her and then remembered that she had no idea what sort of vehicle Scott drove. If he was already there, she would have no way of knowing.

She sucked in her stomach, pulled her shoulders back and strode across the parking lot to the entrance of the shop. No time like the present, she thought as she pulled open the heavy door and stepped inside.

"Penelope!"

She turned at the sound of her name.

Scott was smiling and waving, from a small table tucked away in the corner of the shop.

Whew, Penelope thought, as she waved back and began to weave her way through the room. Every time she saw him, he just got easier and easier on the eyes.

"Hi," she said when she arrived at his table.

He quickly stood up and held out her chair, making her flush with pleasure. My God, he looked fantastic. He'd changed from his jogging clothes and was wearing dark, charcoal grey, dress pants and an electric blue, collared, dress shirt. He was stunning.

"A gentleman, thank you," she said, as she sat down.

Scott's grin was warm as he sat down beside her. "My mother raised me right."

Penelope beamed and tried to concentrate, despite the fact that she could feel the side of his thigh gently pressed up next to hers. "Well, do tell her that I appreciate it," she said, and then could have kicked herself. "Not that I'm saying that you have to talk about me, with your Mother --"

Scott laughed, saving her from herself, and placed his hand lightly on hers, on the table. "No, it's okay, I got what you meant."

He gave her fingers a subtle squeeze and then removed his hand. Penelope wanted to leave her own, glued in place, just in case he felt the need to hold it, again.

"So," she said, glancing at the shop around them. "This is a nice place."

"You've never been?"

"No," Penelope shook her head as she took in the wooden floors, red brick walls and open beamed ceiling. "It's interesting, I like it."

Scott nodded and leaned his elbows on the mosaic tiled table. "Yeah, I've been coming here for a while. They have great coffee and the ambience is just right. Not too mainstream. A good place to be private and have a conversation."

Penelope nodded, at a loss for a response. She'd didn't really put that much thought into a coffee shop, but, then, it had been years since she'd needed a place to meet someone. Privately. She fidgeted in her seat, suddenly uncomfortable at the idea that she was using a coffee shop for more than just coffee.

"So, anything in particular that you feel like?"

"Pardon?" Penelope looked at him, confused.

"Coffee?" Scott gestured toward a board hung on a wall. Lists of coffees and snacks were written boldly across it, very difficult to miss. "Do you have a preference?"

"Oh!" Penelope blushed, thankful that he couldn't read her thoughts, and looked at the board. "Right, coffee. Um, something with vanilla is always nice."

"Done. Something with vanilla, coming up."

He stood up and walked over to the counter to order. Penelope glanced down at their table, determined not to watch. The words that Cameron had spoken to her earlier that morning, "He's not like Uncle Ben," had begun to reverberate in her head and she needed to take a breath.

It's just business, she coached herself, hoping that if she kept saying it, she'd believe it.

"He can just be so bloody clueless, sometimes," Renee said, while darting efficiently around her country-styled kitchen.

"They all can," Kris responded, and then coughed energetically into the phone.

Renee involuntarily pulled back, not that she was going to get anywhere when her headset was strapped firmly to her ear.

"Sorry," Kris said.

"It's okay," Renee replied. "Aside from the coughing, how are you feeling?"

"Actually, even though it doesn't sound like it, surprisingly much better." Kris blew her nose. "I think the worst of it is over, my energy is coming back."

"Well, that's good, because," Renee hesitated and then decided to dive right in. "Honestly, Kris, I need you."

Kris laughed and the laugh turned into a cough. She took a drink of water and caught her breath. "You sound so serious!" She said, trying to skirt the conversation. "What about Pen, she's doing a good job, right?"

"Oh, yeah, I guess," Renee reluctantly agreed, as she pulled a bowl from a drawer and, then, carrots from her fridge. "But, we've only just started on this project and since the contract involves Single Dad ... Who, by the way, is freaking gorgeous!"

"Really? He's that good looking?"

"Believe it." Renee assured her, then pulled her grater from her cupboard and started on the first carrot. "The guy is seriously something. Tall, dark hair, hazel eyes, broad shoulders, the whole deal. He's got that *it* thing, you know? He could give Johnny Depp a run for his money in smoldering sex appeal."

"Wow."

"Yeah, wow, and then some." Renee paused, her carrot poised above her grater. "And, between you and me, if this guy gets too familiar, I'm actually a little worried about Penelope and Ben."

"No, really?" Kris said, shocked by Renee's conviction.

"Really," Renee shrugged and resumed grating her carrots.

"Well, Jeez," Kris sniffled. "What are we going to do?"

"What can we do? This whole situation is completely legitimate."

"Yes, but --"

"But, nothing," Renee said. "I've taken the job, so, nothing we can do there."

"Can't you be the one, just this time, to do the contact part of things?"

"No. My time is being stretched, as it is. Hell, I'm snapping at Paul for opening his mouth. That's another reason why I wish it were you working with me on this one."

"Why? Because I don't like attractive men?"

"No," Renee couldn't help but laugh. "Besides, you have one already. Grayson is gorgeous and you know it. He and Single Dad are in different leagues."

"So," Kris pressed. "We're talking Johnny Depp versus, who?"

"Oh, for goodness sake!" Renee snickered and placed the grater into the carrot bowl and wiped her hands on a dish towel. "Versus, I don't know ... Bradley Cooper!"

"Oooh," Kris said. "You know, you're right on the money there. Grayson does actually look like a slightly more mature Bradley Cooper."

"I know," Renee said. "Now, can I get back to my point? I'm not just saying I need you, to make you feel better. I honestly think that I'm at a point where I cannot continue without a full-time assistant. A partner, really."

"Oh. Well --"

"No, don't go, 'well'," Renee insisted. "I wouldn't make this up! The company is getting too big for me and I need help. Otherwise, there will be a whole lot more snapping at Paul going on, when it's my guilt, not his kindness, that's the problem."

"I don't know," Kris began, and then noisily blew her nose into a tissue.

"Just think about it, okay?" Renee pleaded. "I know that you're feeling dragged out right now, but, when you're feeling better, you'll see that it's a perfect fit. We'll set things up right, you can work around your family, set your hours and all of that. It won't be awkward, it will be just like whenever you've helped me before, only you'll actually get a title and a wage." She smiled into the phone. "We'll have fun. It's a win-win situation!"

"Okay, fine." Kris relented, as she reached for a lozenge, the cellophane crinkling loudly into the phone. "I'll think about it."

"Promise?"

"Yes, I promise." Kris blew her nose, again. "I'm going to go now and make some tea."

"Do you want me to ask Paul to get the boys for you after school?"

"No, thanks," Kris replied. "Didn't I mention? Pen took them this morning and she's going to pick them up, too."

"Yay!" Renee cheered. "Does this mean you guys have worked things out?"

"Very possibly." Kris yawned. "Grayson was the one to actually talk to her this morning and she passed along the message that she's not mad anymore, so --"

"Thank goodness!" Renee enthused. "I'm so relieved, I cannot tell you. I'm sure when you get a chance to talk in person, you'll work out the rest of it and we can all forget it."

"Yeah, you're probably right. You're right about every other darn thing, so, no reason why you wouldn't be about this one, too."

"Finally, someone who's willing to say it! Can I quote you on that?" Renee laughed.

Kris laughed and then coughed.

"Okay," Renee said. "I've got cakes to make and you have vitamin C and tea waiting, so, I'm letting you go to get some rest. I need my assistant, or, rather, my *partner*, ready and able as soon as possible."

"Ren --" Kris cautioned.

"I know, I know," Renee said, before hanging up the phone. "Just think about it."

Scott threw his head back and laughed. Penelope watched him with a combination of delight and guilt.

"God, that's too funny!" Scott said as he wiped his eyes and drank the last of his coffee.

"Well, it's all true," Penelope said. "I couldn't make Bosco up if I tried."

Scott shook his head. "Well, over the top or not, the guy clearly has skills." He let his eyes travel down from the top of her newly colored hair, across her torso and back up to meet her eyes. "You look beautiful."

Penelope blushed and averted her eyes to look at her coffee cup. "Thank you."

Scott watched her, delighted by her reaction. "So, tell me about the new ride I saw you in at the school. Is it yours or ..."

"Yes," Penelope quickly confirmed. "It's mine."

"Wow," Scott nodded. "Quite the change from the Volvo."

Penelope smiled. "Yeah, well, as you found out the other day, it was time for an upgrade."

"Oh, I don't know," Scott's face grew thoughtful as he leaned back in his chair. "I think that that car was a dream."

Penelope raised an eyebrow.

"If it hadn't had its door locking quirk," he said, looking her right in the eye. "I'd never have stopped and met you. And, that would have been a serious shame."

Penelope cleared her throat and swallowed. Mayday, mayday, she was in over her head.

"I may just have to go and buy it, now," Scott said, a slow grin spreading across his face. "So that I can display it in my driveway as a memento of how we met."

Penelope burst out laughing. "Or, you could just go over to the car lot and take a picture of it to hang from your keychain!"

Scott joined her in her laughter and looked at her with appreciation. Adorable, cute and funny. Quite the combination. He wondered if her fiancé really knew what he held in his grasp.

Penelope took a peek at her watch and gasped. "Oh, hell, is that really the time? Sorry, but, I'm going to have to take off. I have to pick up Cameron right away."

Scott looked at his own watch and nodded. "I've got to get back to work, too."

Penelope stood up and Scott followed her lead. She stepped by him, caught a hint of his cologne and felt the desire to stop and sniff him. Closely.

"Listen," he said as they left the coffee shop, side by side. "I really enjoyed this and, even though we talked about a lot of things besides the catering job, there might still be stuff I need to pass along."

"Oh, of course!" Penelope eagerly agreed. "There could be loads of details to discuss, before the actual day that the cakes need to be completed."

"Yes. Exactly," Scott affirmed. "That's what I'm saying."

"You have my card, right?"

"Right."

"So, you can just call me, on my cell phone, whenever you need for us to talk, or meet, or whatever ..."

"That's what I was thinking, too," Scott jumped in. "Instead of bothering Renee, I could just continue to call you directly."

"Because, she's so busy with the actual baking and creating," Penelope finished.

"Exactly," Scott nodded, pleased.

They were at her car and Penelope pulled her keys from her bag. She looked him in the eye and tried her best not to fidget and shuffle her feet like a nervous child. "Okay, well, I really should run. Thanks again, for coffee, and, well, everything."

It was my pleasure, Penelope." Scott smiled and laid his hand gently on her shoulder. "Really."

Penelope's breath caught in her chest and her knees felt weak at his touch. A tremor of excitement, mixed with a bit of fear, ran through her. She didn't know exactly what she was doing, but, even still, she didn't want it to stop.

"I'll talk to you soon, then?" She dared to ask.

"Definitely," Scott nodded and let his hand drop from her shoulder. "Absolutely."

Ben rubbed his hands together in anticipation when he heard the sound of the garage door. Penelope was home, which meant that his timing was perfect. The moment he heard the house door open, he called out, "Hey, Pen! I'm in the kitchen!"

Penelope paused in the doorway and inhaled deeply. Thai food. Her absolute favorite. She pulled off her shoes and hurried into the kitchen, all smiles. Ben's grin widened when he saw her reaction. "Welcome home!"

"What are you doing?"

"What does it look like?" Ben replied. "I'm making a surprise dinner for my beautiful fiancée. Got a problem with that?"

Penelope giggled. "What's the occasion?"

Ben affected a hurt look. "Occasion? There has to be an *occasion* for me to make a delicious meal for my heart's desire?"

Penelope raised an eyebrow and Ben laughed. "Okay, okay, you've got a point, a little over the top. However," he insisted, as he strode into the adjoining family room and turned around to face her, his arms wide like a politician. "The only occasion I can think of is, I think you're wonderful and special and I want you to remember that I feel that way."

Penelope swallowed uncomfortably. She'd just spend the greater part of the afternoon with Scott and here was Ben, kind and generous Ben, cooking for her. "Well, in that case," she followed in his footsteps and pulled him close. "Thank you."

Ben wrapped his arms snugly around her waist. "You're welcome," he said, his voice husky with desire. He leaned in to kiss her and Penelope pressed herself against his firm torso. Ben groaned and ran his hands down her back pulling her tightly against his groin.

"Your dinner," Penelope broke their kiss and gestured to the kitchen.

"Can wait." Ben stated, firmly, and ran his hands up under her shirt to find the clasp on her bra.

It was Penelope's turn to groan as Ben freed the clasp and then ran his hands around to the front of her shirt to cup her full breasts. Her knees buckle slightly when he kissed her neck and caressed her with a practiced touch.

"Yes," she said, her breath coming in short gasps. "It can wait."

When Ben peeled her shirt from her shoulders, Penelope paused for the briefest of moments, remembering Scott's hand in the exact same spot. She quickly forced the thought away and focused upon her fiancé.

"No other thoughts," she murmured, to herself, as she reveled in the heat from Ben's kisses, traveling down her stomach.

"What?" Ben paused, his mouth poised just inches from his next target.

"Nothing," Penelope stammered. "Just you."

Ben grinned and gently pulled her down to the soft rug beneath them.

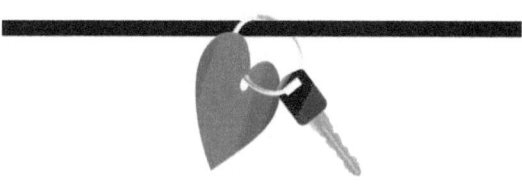

Six

"So, this is what the people in the land of the living are doing, huh?" Kris said as she walked beside Penelope into a clothing store. It was lunch hour, midweek, and the two women were taking advantage of the quiet mall traffic. "Man, I'm glad that that cold is behind me. It feels really good to be out of the house."

Penelope grinned, as she strode over to a discount rack. "Yup, while you were laid up in bed, the world continued shopping."

"From the sounds of it," Kris said, her voice sly and suggestive. "I wouldn't say I was the only one who was in a 'laid' state!"

Penelope laughed out loud and then clapped her hand over her mouth when other shoppers glanced her way. "I'm telling you, the past few days, I don't know what's gotten into Ben --"

"Or, better yet, what Ben's gotten into!"

Penelope gave her a playful shove. "Stop! You'll make me blush!" She shook her head and Kris giggled. "But, really, the man is acting like a teenager!"

"Second childhood?" Kris offered, as she pulled a silky, dark purple, blouse from the rack and held it up in front of her slim body. "Is this my color?"

Penelope raised an eyebrow at Kris. Honestly, the woman was so gorgeous, anything was her color. Dressed in slim fitting jeans, knee high, black boots and a blouse patterned in swirls of yellow and orange, she looked like a model.

"Maybe, maybe not," Kris debated on the blouse.

"If I was to guess, off the top of my head," Penelope said, as she pushed the hangers on the rack back and forth, flitting from one blouse, to the next. "I think it might be because I said something about us being an old married couple."

Kris turned her attention from the blouse and chuckled. "Oh. Okay. Now his behavior makes sense. When did you tell him that?"

"It was after our misunderstanding at your place," Penelope gestured back and forth, between them. "I was angry about our miscommunication and, then, when he was so surprised by my makeover, I lashed out at him and told him that that we were like an old married couple, stuck in our ruts."

Kris nodded. "Huh. Maybe I'll have to try that out on Grayson."

Penelope couldn't help but laugh. "Go for it. The magic trick for the Miller brothers. Just mention old and married, and watch out!"

"Oooh, these are nice," Kris gestured to some elaborate, silver earrings, hanging on a jewelry display rack. "With your new hair, they'd look great on you."

"So, what about you," Penelope examined the earrings. "What's the magic trick that would work on you?"

"What do you mean?"

Penelope gave up on examining the earrings, put them back on the rack and sighed. "I know that you've been feeling a bit out of sorts, yourself." She held up her hand to silence Kris' protests. "No, don't even try to deny it. Renee and I talked."

"I'm fine," Kris said, matter-of-fact.

"Right. Whatever." Penelope flicked some lint from her houndstooth dress pants. She would never have believed that she could get away with such a pattern, but, the salesgirl who had helped her buy them, had proved her wrong. "I'm not arguing with you on that, but, I will say that Renee is absolutely not fine. I'm sure you've noticed it, too."

Kris rolled her eyes and, reluctantly, nodded.

"She's seriously suffering from frayed nerves," Penelope went on. "I'm worried for her. That's why, there's no question that she really does need you and, I think, if you're honest with yourself, you'll see that you need to take the job."

"Pen, you don't understand," Kris stated, as she pushed her red curls back from her face.

Penelope faced Kris. "Want to get out of here and keep on looking?"

Kris nodded and replaced the purple blouse back on its hanger.

"Okay," Penelope said, as they walked out of the store empty handed. "Explain it to me, then. What is it I don't understand?"

"I don't want a job out of pity." Kris said, and then shook her head when Penelope pulled a face. "And, don't say it isn't pity, because Grayson offered me a job at his company, too. I didn't accept it, for the same reason I'm not sure about Renee."

Penelope stopped walking and sighed. Kris was reacting exactly as Renee had predicted she would. It was, clearly, going to be an uphill battle. "Okay, fine, you see it as pity. Or, nepotism. Or, both. But, did you ever think, for a moment, that you might be wrong? That Grayson offered you a job because you'd be an asset to his team? Or, that Renee wants you to be her partner for the same reasons?"

Kris nodded and fiddled with the zipper on her black, quilted gilet. "I know. And, obviously, I have had those thoughts. But, I want to ... I *need* to, get my own job, first. A separate job. Then, at least, I'll have proved to myself that I can actually be hired, without family ties."

"Fine." Penelope said and crossed her arms, fed up. "Then, do it, already."

"Do what?"

"Put your money where your mouth is. Get a job, some job that will do your proving, and get it out of your system and get on with it!"

Kris looked at Penelope, incredulously. "And, where do you suggest I go to get this job, huh?"

Penelope looked around and pointed to an adjacent coffee shop. "There! Go there and apply. I dare you!"

Kris started to laugh and Penelope looked victorious. "You see! You won't do it, you're just talking a lot of blather --"

Kris rounded on Penelope. "I didn't say I wouldn't do it, I just found it funny!" She pushed Penelope aside. "Get out of my way and wait here!"

Penelope watched, open mouthed, as Kris marched across the corridor, her knee high boots clomping on the tiled floor, and into the coffee shop. A few minutes passed, then a few more, and Penelope began to wonder if Kris had just sat down to coffee and was leaving her to wait and suffer, when her friend emerged from the shop, looking triumphant.

"Ha! There, done!"

"What? What's done?" Penelope asked, taken aback.

Kris stood tall and proud, her hair flowing like shiny, red waves down her slim back. "I got the job, it's mine. I start tomorrow afternoon."

"Oh-my-God! There was actually a position for hire?"

"Yup!"

"And you applied for it?" Penelope was reeling and feeling slightly faint.

"Yup!" Kris beamed.

"You did not!"

"Yes I did!"

Penelope could not believe it. "Seriously? You're messing with me, right?" Penelope waited a beat, but, Kris didn't so much as flinch. "My God, Kris, are you nuts? What about the boys? You'll probably have to work shifts. That is, I'm assuming, if you're waiting tables and not washing the dishes --"

"Yes, I'm waiting tables," Kris gave her a scathing look. "And, no worries about the shifts. I told them that I'm available in the daytime, during school hours, and on weekends, and they were fine with that."

"Great. Wonderful. They were fine with that," Penelope repeated, as she walked with a heavy heart beside her glowing friend.

What had she done? The coffee shop might have said that they were fine with Kris', supposedly, available hours, but, Penelope had a sinking feeling that Grayson wouldn't be anywhere near as accommodating.

"No. Absolutely not." Grayson stated, bluntly. He stood wide-legged, his arms folded across his broad chest, and glared at his wife.

"No?" Kris reiterated, her neck rolling as she fixed Grayson with a wide-eyed stare. "You're saying, '*no*,' as though you have any say in the matter?"

The muscles in Grayson's jaw flexed as he clenched his teeth and tried to keep his temper. It was the end of a very long work day, they had finally got their boys off to bed, and all that he really wanted was to take a breather and relax on the couch. So much for that idea.

"That's right, Kris," he said, his nostrils flaring from his effort to keep his patience. "And, as a matter of fact, I do have some say. It affects me, too."

"How? How does my working, in the daytime, I might add, when you are at work and the boys are at school, affect *you*?"

"Jesus," Grayson exploded and ran his hands through his dark blonde hair. So much for patience. "You get these ideas and you're just so damned stubborn sometimes. It's infuriating!"

Kris glared at him. "Oh, so I'm '*stubborn*' when I want to have a job that pays me and gives me an identity, besides that of someone's Mom, or wife?"

"That is not what I said."

Kris ignored him and nodded, furious. "Right. Got it. So, by law of deduction, I'd be considered reasonable, as long as I stay working here all day, doing your God-damned laundry?"

"That's not what I said!" Grayson insisted, as he started pacing the length of the kitchen.

"It sure sounded like --"

"No! Just shut up and listen!"

"Oh!" She pointed a rigid finger at him. "Don't you dare tell me to shut up!"

Grayson took a deep breath and turned to face his wife. "Okay, fine. I'm sorry. But, still, sometimes, Kris, you need to shut your mouth and listen."

Kris narrowed her eyes at him, but stayed quiet.

"I absolutely understand why you want to have something of your own, outside this house. I get that. But, seriously, Hon, waiting tables is not the answer."

"That's not for you to say --"

Grayson held up his hand and Kris shut her mouth, again. "I think that you just got this job to prove a point."

"No," Kris blurted, then bit her lip to stop herself from interrupting, further.

"Yes," Grayson said, looking her in the eye. "And, the thing is, Kris, we all know that you are talented as hell. Me, the boys, heck, the whole family."

Kris sighed and let her eyes slide away, to look at her finger nails.

He reached out and touched her shoulder. "Which is why we - meaning me, Penelope and Renee - have been encouraging you to consider working for Renee."

Kris shook her head and looked up from her hands. "Thank you, but, I disagree. Her offer is pity based and I know it."

Grayson dropped his hand from her shoulder and shook his head, incredulous. "It is not pity, in any way, at all! Renee really does need help, it's getting away from her, and if you could just grow up for a moment -_"

Kris looked at him, wide-eyed with shock.

"Oh, yeah, I said it," Grayson insisted as he stared her down. "If you, *Kristine*, could just grow up and stop acting like our six year old son and look past yourself for a minute, you'd see that Renee needs your special skills and talents. Not out of pity, but, legitimate need."

Kris glared at him. She couldn't get past his comment that she needed to 'grow up'. "Oh, fine, mister-have-all-the-answers. You think you're so smart? Well, find an answer for this one. GO-TO-HELL!"

She whirled around and stormed out of the kitchen.

Grayson sighed and leaned against the kitchen counter. She was a firecracker, no doubt about it. Experience had shown him that she'd come around, eventually. He just hoped that, for all of their sakes, it was sooner than later.

Ben tapped his pen on his desk and listened to the sound of Penelope's phone ringing in his ear. She wasn't answering. He had been hoping to catch her, to suggest that they meet for dinner.

He let it go all the way to her voicemail, before he hung up. He'd try her, again, when he'd shut everything down for the day.

"Well, it sounds like," Scott observed, leaning in toward Penelope as he spoke. "Between work and your family, you lead a very full life."

"I suppose so," Penelope smiled.

She was seated across from Scott, at a candle lit table in an intimate Italian restaurant, having coffee and not much else. Not from Scott's lack of trying.

"Are you sure you just want a coffee?" He gestured to the closed menus on their table. "When I called you and asked you to meet me, I really did want to buy you dinner."

Penelope hesitated. Coffee was one thing, dinner was another. Besides, she hadn't told Ben that she was going to be late, never mind going to miss dinner.

"Maybe just an appetizer?" He encouraged. "They make a delicious bruschetta."

"No, really," she stammered, meeting his eye and then swiftly looking away. "I shouldn't. My, umm, well, I didn't tell anyone that I was going to be late, so ..."

Scott nodded. Ahh. Got it. "Okay," he said, warmly. "No problem. If you only have time for coffee, then that's what I'll take."

"Not that I'm not glad that you called," Penelope added. "I mean, obviously, you had to call because of the project, but --"

"But," Scott finished, for her. "I could have just called and relayed the information. I didn't have to set up an actual date, Penelope. I wanted to see you, too."

Penelope shifted uncomfortably in her seat. He said date. Eeek. While she wanted it to be true, and had been a bit giddy with excitement when he had called, she wasn't sure how comfortable she was actually facing it, head on.

"What I'm saying is," Scott clarified. "I'm happy that this has given me a chance to get to know you a bit better and develop a ... friendship."

"Oh, me, too!" Penelope tripped over her own words in her haste to agree. "Good friends! We all need friends, right?"

She nodded enthusiastically and exhaled a shaky, relieved breath. She could privately think lascivious thoughts, secure in the fact that he was thinking friendly ones. That was okay.

Scott smiled warmly, glad that she had relaxed, and gestured to her cup. "More coffee, before we head out?"

"None for me, thanks," Penelope said and reached for her purse, her engagement ring glittering wildly in the soft lights surrounding them.

"Whoa," he said, placing his hand firmly over top of hers. "That wasn't a hint. *I* issued the invitation, *I* pay."

Penelope looked at his hand over hers, her ring pressed between them, and then up to his dark and welcoming eyes. "If you're sure," was all that she was able to muster.

"Of course I am," Scott replied, matter-of-factly. "I apologize, but, that old fashioned ideal is rearing its head. Where I come from, when a man issues an invitation, he pays."

Penelope nodded and when he pulled his hand from hers, it took all of her will power not to grab it back.

"Will I see you again, do you think?" She blurted, before she chickened out.

Scott reached into his pocket for his wallet and grinned, his eyes twinkling with pleasure at the question. "I'd like that. Very much."

Penelope watched as he threw some bills on the table, and then stood up from her chair. Scott followed her lead.

"I'm sure" he told her. "I can easily find some sort of reason why I need to pass on more information for this baking project."

Penelope laughed and let him help her with her red trench coat.

"Let me have a chat with my boss," he said as he pulled on his chocolate brown, leather jacket. It made his broad shoulders look even wider. "I'm sure I'll be calling you right away. Who knows, maybe it will be enough information, that we'll actually need to meet for drinks and dinner."

Penelope flushed and ducked her head to gather her purse into her hands. Her ring sparkled defiantly at her, again. Daring her to ignore it.

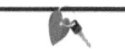

"I'm really sorry," Renee said, into Paul's chest.

He held her securely in his arms and spoke into the short, dark hair at the top of her head. "No, it was my fault. I know that you're under a lot of pressure and I should have remembered that. It makes complete sense, to me, why you got angry."

Renee smiled. Trust her husband to take the blame for a situation that was clearly her fault. "I have a feeling you're not going to let me take the blame for this one."

"Good call."

Renee tilted back in his arms, freeing her face from the soft fleece of his pullover, and laughed up at him. "You're too good to me, Paul Miller."

Paul leaned in and planted a slow, sensuous kiss on her mouth. When he pulled back, leaving Renee looking a bit dazed, he grinned. "I'm the lucky one here. We both know it."

"Oh, no," she began, before he silenced her with another kiss.

When they came up for air, he caressed her lips with the tip of his finger and nodded. "You're my dream come true, Ren. There's not one day that goes by that I don't know it."

Renee grinned, a mischievous glint in her eye, and grabbed his hand. "Well, then," she said, as she pulled him toward their bedroom. "Don't let me stop you from sharing your dream!"

Paul laughed and chased her into the room. Sometimes, a bit of tension was the best thing for a marriage.

Penelope turned her car into her garage and cut the engine. Ben's car was parked in its normal spot and Penelope swallowed, uneasily. She was feeling a mixture of guilt and dread about seeing her fiancé and it was causing the coffee she had drank earlier to churn uncomfortably in her stomach.

"Damn it," she exhaled, under her breath. Why had she not taken a moment to pull her cell phone from the depths of her purse, when she was sitting opposite Scott, in the restaurant? That was all she would have had to do, to avoid having three - yes, three - unanswered messages from Ben, waiting for her.

Instead, she'd left her phone to swim at the bottom of her bag, and then had to spend her entire drive home, turning over plausible stories as to why she hadn't been available to take his call, nor even see his messages, until it was too late. Things were starting to get complicated.

Penelope stepped out of her car and walked with trepidation toward the door. I should have never agreed to meet Scott, after dark, she silently chastised herself. Daytime was one thing, evening was a whole other animal.

She unlocked the door and stepped into the house, pulled off her new, suede boots and listened for ... anything. There was nothing.

"Hello?" She called out, as she padded on stocking feet toward the kitchen. "Ben?"

Penelope scanned the kitchen. It was clear to her, by the pans in the sink, that Ben had made himself something to eat. So, where the heck was he?

Penelope pulled off her jacket and laid it across the back of a chair, looked around for a note and, then, she heard it. The sound of water from the shower in their en-suite, upstairs. Bingo. She'd found him.

"Might be good, might be bad," she muttered to herself, stretching her neck from side to side.

Penelope knew that, if Ben was inclined to shower at the end of the day, it could mean one of two things. The first, he'd had an exhausting day at work and needed to let the whole thing wash down the drain. Or, the second, he was upset and needed the feel of the hot water on his skin to relax and gain some relativity. Penelope sincerely hoped it was the former.

Her cell phone rang, from the depths of her purse, and Penelope didn't miss the irony. Sure, she thought, as she fished it from her bag. Now I hear it. She checked the caller ID, it was Scott. Shit.

Penelope took a breath and pressed the button, "Hello?" She kept her voice low and moved away from the kitchen, into the family room.

"Penelope?"

"Yes?" She almost whispered, as she listened for the sound of running water with her free ear. The shower had stopped. She had to hurry.

"It's Scott. You sound strange, are we getting a bad reception? Should I call back?"

"No!" Penelope blurted, and then cringed at the volume of her voice. She moved further into the family room, slid open the patio door to their deck and slipped outside.

"Oh," Scott said. "That's better. I can hear you now."

Come *on*, she thought, fidgeting back and forth, from one stocking clad foot to the next. It's cold and I don't have time for this. Tell me why you're calling.

"So, you're probably wondering why I'm calling, when I just saw you," Scott said, his voice friendly.

"Sure," Penelope replied, faking a casual tone. "What's up?"

"I just remembered that there was something I didn't mention at the restaurant --"

Penelope was watching through the glass of the patio door for Ben and when she saw his shadow on the stairs, she missed Scott's words, completely. "Hell!" She hissed, feeling cornered.

"Pardon?" Scott asked, sounding very confused.

While Ben hadn't seen her through the glass, Penelope knew he'd quickly notice her jacket in the kitchen. She had to think fast. "Sorry, just dropped a ... glass!"

"Oh, Jeez," Scott said. "Are you okay?"

"Yes! I'm fine," Penelope knew she had to hurry them along. "But, I should go and get this cleaned up. Sorry ..."

"No, no," Scott said. "I totally understand. Just tell Renee, the boss wants two more cakes added, for his daughters."

"Done," Penelope stated and resisted the urge to abruptly hang up.

"I'll email you the info and, then, be in touch soon--"

Penelope watched as, sure enough, Ben noticed her jacket on the back of the kitchen chair. He glanced around with a curious expression on his face.

"Gotta run!" She cut Scott off. "Sorry! Talk soon!" She pressed end and exhaled, feeling slightly nauseous.

Ben moved from the kitchen to the family room, just as she put her hand on the patio door and pushed it open.

"Hey!" He said, surprised. "I saw your jacket and was wondering where you'd disappeared to."

Penelope smiled and tried not to shiver as she slipped into the house, closing the door firmly behind her. "I thought I heard a noise and was just checking it out. It was nothing. False alarm."

"Did you get my messages?" Ben asked, gesturing to the cell phone, still in her grasp.

"I did," Penelope said, pulling a disappointed face. "I'm sorry I didn't hear my phone when you called. Somehow the ringer got turned off, maybe when it was in my purse. It wasn't until I was in the car, at a light, that I checked and I was already on my way home ..."

Ben waved his hand dismissively. "Don't worry about it, it happens."

Penelope silently cheered. She was in the clear. He believed her story, she was shutting up while she was ahead.

"Did you stop for anything to eat?"

"No," she said, crossing the fingers of her left hand behind her back. She wasn't lying, she hadn't eaten at the Italian restaurant. "I left the office and came right home."

Okay, that one was a lie.

"Well, then," Ben smiled lovingly at her. "Let's get you fed."

Penelope let her shoulders relax and watched as he turned toward the kitchen. She felt as though she had dodged a bullet and, yet, instead of revealing in the relief, she was feeling ... embarrassed.

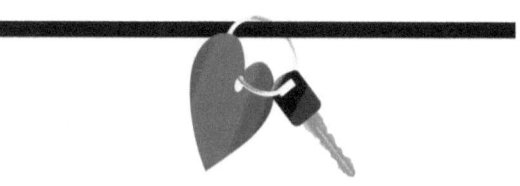

SEVEN

I really don't know what to say, Pen," Renee stated, while she tacked a sketch of a sewing-themed cake onto a large cork board in her home office. "It sounds like you're really giving a lot of attention to this project, so, maybe ... thank you?"

Penelope cocked her head at the question in Renee's tone. "What's wrong? You sound unsure."

Renee sighed and placed a hand on her hip. She gestured, with her free hand, to the multiple cake sketches tacked up in the board. The chaos on the board matched the clutter and disarray of her office. "Well, clearly, I have a whole hell of a lot of work to do with these cakes. So, I would hope that it's obvious that

I appreciate all of the info you've gathered about them. However, that being said --"

Penelope leaned forward when Renee hesitated, waiting for her to finish.

Renee took a deep breath and brazened forward. "I'm a little worried that spending so much time with Scott could be detrimental to your ..."

Penelope waited, again. Then, when Renee began to play with the pleats on her yellow, knee length, skirt, instead of looking her in the eye, she prompted. "Detrimental to my what, Renee? Spit it out."

"Your home life." Renee exhaled, and clenched the cotton of her skirt in her hand. She was glad to have said it, but, was bracing herself for the response.

Penelope was taken aback. She hadn't expected that. She slowly folded her arms across her chest, determined to keep her cool. "Okay," she shrugged her shoulders. "Fair enough. I can see how you'd get that. How you'd feel that way. But, there's nothing to be concerned about, so, --"

"Really?" Renee rounded on Penelope, her voice practically dripping with skepticism. "Is that really the truth? Because, honestly, Pen, I'm thinking that there might be a *lot* to be concerned about."

Penelope shook back her auburn curls, smoothed the front of her green, V-neck blouse and shook her head. "That's ridiculous," she said, finally.

"Then, please, tell me," Renee continued, one eyebrow raised as she reflexively started to move things around on her desk. "Why it is, in the last 20 minutes, all I've heard from you is, 'Scott this,' and, 'Scott that'. I honestly don't even remember the last time you mentioned Ben. Don't you have a wedding that needs to be planned?"

Penelope cleared her throat and swallowed. "I'm not sure what my wedding has to do with any of this, since we're talking about the cake job."

"Pen," Renee shot her a wry look.

"However," Penelope ignored her. "If you must know, Ben and I haven't really been pushing that forward. I think he wants more time."

Renee stared incredulously at Penelope. "Oh, come *on*," she said, throwing her hands in the air. "There is no way that Ben is getting cold feet! He would have done the deed months ago and you know it!"

Penelope twisted away from Renee and her knowing expression. She fixed her gaze on some dog toys scattered on the floor. "Look, I don't think it is our place to presume any of Ben's feelings --"

"Oh, *Penelope*!" Renee barked and stamped her foot, making Penelope jump. "Until you get honest with yourself, let's just leave this alone, okay?"

"What?" Penelope spun on her heel to face Renee.

"I'm not playing this banter game with you," Renee cut her off. "Quite frankly, I'm too old, not to mention way too busy, for this, and so are you. It's time to face whatever you've got going on and deal with it."

Penelope pressed her lips together and nodded. She couldn't argue. Not with any sort of conviction. It was a waste of her breath. Renee was right, she really did have to sort out where her thoughts and feelings were. Quickly.

"Okay," Renee yawned and massaged her temples. "Let's go and check my email and see what those changes are, for the cakes. You have to get back to work and this project isn't going to create itself."

"Oh, *Miss?*"

Kris turned slowly on the heel of her boot and narrowed her eyes at the petulant, greasy, eyebrow-pierced teenager, raising his coffee cup in her direction.

"I asked for nutmeg on this, *remember?*"

Kris breathed deeply and counted to ten in her head to keep her cool. If one of her children had used such a blatantly sarcastic tone with her, or anyone else for that matter, she would have slapped that child across the backside and sent him to his room. She shook her long, red hair, inwardly reminded herself that she was doing her job, and got control of her face. "Right," she said, with false sincerity. "I *do* remember. I'll be right back."

She marched back to the coffee counter, where they stored the spices, and took another deep breath. It was only her first day, her feet were starting to ache in her patent leather, ankle boots and, already, she had lost her patience with people. When had humanity become so rude? She was utterly shocked at the general, it's-my-due attitude. Especially amongst the teenagers. Forget respect, they seemed to be working hard at developing their apathy.

Kris picked up the nutmeg and, as she turned away from the counter, could not believe what she was hearing, echoing across the coffee shop, from her customer's mouth.

"Seriously," Petulant teen lamented, loudly, while he twisted one of the many earrings in his over-pierced ear. "Clearly, getting *old* doesn't mean getting *smart!*"

He grinned at his own wit and Kris saw red. She'd taken the time on her hair and make up for this? Enough was enough.

"Your nutmeg?" She said, striding fast across the floor to tower over him.

Petulant teen looked up, startled.

Kris glared at him, held the jar aloft and began not to sprinkle, but, instead, violently shake the contents of it into his coffee. Then, for good measure, she scattered the rest of it into his lap, making him leap to his feet, shocked to his core.

"What the hell is *wrong* with you?!" Petulant teen screeched. He pawed at his shirt and pants, trying in vain to brush away the dark, staining, powder. It didn't work, he just made it worse.

Kris slammed the near empty jar onto his table, making his companion scramble to her feet to get out of the line of fire. "What's *wrong*? Really? You want to know what's wrong?"

"You --" He sputtered. That was as far as he got, before Kris cut him off.

"To start," she stared him down, her teeth gritted and eyes blazing. "You are an inconsiderate, sniffling, little creep, who seems to have no respect for anyone besides yourself. And, by looking at the state of you," she stared pointedly at his unkempt clothing and multiple piercings. "Even *that's* questionable."

"You're nuts, lady!" Petulant teen blurted, his eyes practically bulging.

Kris looked at the child before her and couldn't help but snicker. "You think *this* is nuts? Wait until you get married. " She smirked at the very idea. "Not that anyone would have you --"

"WHAT is going on here?"

Kris jerked and spun around to take in the shocked face of her manager. She was a young girl - well, probably in her early twenties - but, as far as Kris was concerned, young.

"We've had a bit of an accident," Kris began.

"No!" Petulant teen sputtered. "That was NOT an accident!"

He waved his hands in frustration at his stained clothes and Kris noticed that his companion looked more than a little amused.

"That was on purpose!" He pointed his finger, first at Kris, and then everyone else in his immediate vicinity. "Everyone saw it! Your *insane* employee just lost her mind and poured nutmeg all over me!" His voice was beginning to squeak and take on a distinctive whine. "On *purpose!*"

The manager turned to Kris and asked, her voice grave and serious. "Is this true?"

Kris stared back at her, aware that every customer in the coffee shop had abandoned their own conversations to listen intently to the drama unfolding. She sighed. What a hassle.

"Well? Is it?" The manager prompted.

"You know," Kris said, and straightened her spine to revel in the fact that she stood taller than both the teen and the manager. "Truth is a strange concept, isn't it? One person's version isn't always another's, I find."

Petulant teen glared at her, ready to offer more commentary. Apparently, he was a drama queen, to boot. What a surprise. Kris held no interest in hearing what he had to say, so, she brushed her hands on the apron tied around her slim waist, pushed past the manager, and made a bee line for the back of the coffee shop. She paused at the staff room doorway, and fixed her eyes on the spice stained teen. "However, I can tell you one thing. Whatever happened here, it set me free. How about you?"

She didn't wait for a reply and spun on her heel to disappear inside the staff room. She had reached her limit, it was time to go. She yanked her purse from a cubby, with her name scrawled across it on masking tape, and started to giggle. The more she replayed the incident in her head, the funnier it became.

Then, when she heard the manager's voice through the closed door, attempting to do damage control, Kris lost it completely. She laughed until tears leaked from her eyes, threatening to ruin her mascara. What the hell had she been thinking?

She caught her breath and regained her composure, pulled her black apron from around her hips with a flourish and tossed it onto the staff room table. She had told the boy that she was free. Time to get on with it.

Penelope wrinkled her nose as she entered the house. Was she smelling paint? And, if so, why? "Ben?" She called out as she walked through the hallway and kitchen, toward the staircase.

"Pen? Is that you?" Ben's voice called out. He sounded excited.

"Yes, what's going on?" She answered as she pulled off her red trench coat. "How come you're home so early?"

"Don't come up! Wait a minute!"

Penelope raised an eyebrow. It was half past five and, usually, Ben didn't arrive home until at least six.

"Okay," Ben called out as he thundered noisily down the staircase.

Penelope smiled and noticed that he was wearing an old pair of jeans and a paint splattered t-shirt. It explained the smell, anyway. "What are you doing? What's going on? Did you go to work today?"

"Come with me," Ben ignored her questions and reached for her hand. "Only, don't look."

Penelope laughed as he led her toward the staircase. "I'm not climbing those with my eyes closed."

Ben followed her gaze and laughed, too. "Okay, okay, fine. But, when we get to the top, then close your eyes."

"Fine."

He held her hand tightly and practically dragged her up the staircase beside him. When they got to the top he pointed at her face. "Close 'em!"

Penelope laughed. "You're being so silly!" When she saw the pleading look on his face, she relented. "Okay, okay, they're closed. Please don't walk me into any walls."

Ben grinned at her, even though Penelope had shut her eyes and couldn't see him, and led her carefully toward their bedroom. He opened the door and yelled, "Tada! Open your eyes!"

"Oh-my-God, Ben!" Penelope blurted, when she opened her eyes. She was amazed. He has transformed their bedroom from plain, to fabulous!

Where once there had been off-white walls, was paint the color of deep, red wine. Their faded, peach-toned bedding had been replaced with puffy pillows and a duvet made up of swirling patterns of forest green, fresh cream and chocolate brown. The final touch was a pair of silver bedside lamps that cast a soft glow over the room. It was all so lush and inviting, Penelope was speechless. Ben had created a perfect lover's hideaway.

"Why? How?" Penelope stammered as she gestured with sweeping arms to the room around them.

"For you," Ben said, simply. "For us. Because, I wanted to. Because, I love you."

Penelope's eyes began to well with tears. It was all so unexpected, she didn't know how to react. "I don't know what to say," she managed to croak.

Ben grinned and wrapped her in a hug. "You don't have to say anything. You just did."

Penelope clung to him and breathed deeply to get hold of herself. She had to stop seeing Scott. Even though nothing had happened, she knew it was true. How could she continue to see him, and feel such unsettling, confusing feelings, and then come home to Ben with a clear conscience?

"What are you thinking?" Ben asked, noticing that she'd gone quiet.

Penelope sniffed loudly and cleared her throat. "I'm thinking I'm one lucky woman," she pulled back to look directly at him. "You did a beautiful thing."

Ben smiled, pleased that his instincts had been correct. "That's all I was hoping for, Sweetie," he said, with a grin. "But, that being said, what do you say to grabbing some dinner while this continues to air out? I'm starting to feel a bit lightheaded."

Penelope nodded. "Good idea. Let me take a minute to clean up," she gestured to her tearstained face.

Ben looked down at his clothes. "No problem, I need to take a quick shower and change first, too." He pulled his t-shirt over his blonde head, revealing his strong, golden torso, and his expression suddenly became sly. "Unless, you feel like joining me?"

Penelope gave one last glance toward their newly made over bedroom and felt a stab of self-loathing when her mind flashed with a mental image of Scott ... hot and naked across the new bedding. She wanted to slap herself. "I'll grab fresh towels," she said, determined to push the thoughts from her head.

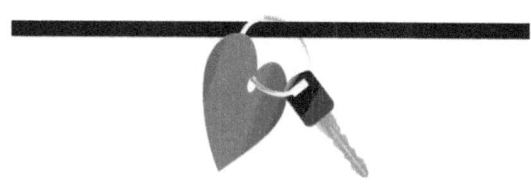

Eight

Renee was doubled over, gasping with laughter. Kris and Penelope had dropped in at lunch time for a visit, and Kris was regaling them with the tale of how she had gotten herself fired on her very first day on the job at the coffee house.

Penelope wiped tears of mirth from her eyes as she grabbed a tissue from a container on the kitchen counter top to blot her nose. "God, that poor kid! He probably still doesn't know what hit him!"

"Poor kid, my ass!" Kris exclaimed, swiveling in her seat at the island. "He's lucky the child-manager showed up when she did, or I would have had him in tears!"

Penelope and Renee burst into a fresh roar of giggles and Kris snickered. It *was* amusing, even though she had lost her job as a result of the incident.

"The ones that I feel most sorry for, truthfully, are my boys," Kris offered, as she picked up her coffee cup. "After that incident, I came home all fired up and, when they came home after school, they got a stern lecture about manners and respect."

"Oh, no," Renee shook her head.

"Yup," Kris grinned. "I don't think that they knew what hit them, but, they were savvy enough to stay quiet and let me say my peace."

"Learned from their Dad," Penelope teased.

"Hey, as long as they're learning," Kris stated with a salute of her cup.

"Well, all I can say is, that smarmy kid will definitely turn and run in the other direction, should he ever lay eyes upon you, again." Penelope shook her head, impressed, then switched gears. "So, now that you're once again without gainful employment, what's your plan?"

Kris shot her a warning look, knowing full well at that which Penelope was hinting. Penelope crossed her legs and stared back, wide-eyed, the picture of innocence.

"Oh, that's right!" Renee jumped in, her silver and blue crystal, dangle earrings, swaying merrily. "That means you're a free agent."

Kris looked at the two eager faces and deflated. Two against one, it was too much. "Well, okay, I *have* been thinking," she began, and then shot another warning look at Penelope to keep her mouth shut. "And, if you still want me --"

"I do! I do!" Renee exclaimed and leaped off of her chair to grab Kris in a hug. "This is going to be fantastic! You'll see! You'll wonder why you didn't join in with me sooner!"

Kris hugged her back and laughed. "Okay, okay," she agreed and then untangled herself from Renee's embrace. "I'm sure you're going to be right."

"She *is* right," Penelope confirmed, and served herself salad from a bowl in the middle of the island. "You guys are going to make a great team. You already have been in the past, so, this will just be even better."

Kris nodded and, then, noticed Penelope's face suddenly cloud over. "What?" She asked, concerned. "What's wrong?"

"What?" Penelope deflected, not meeting Kris' eye.

"You looked really bothered there, for a moment," Kris told her. "Is there something wrong with the salad?"

Renee immediately peered into the bowl, her forehead creased with concern.

"No, the salad's fine," Penelope waved her hand dismissively. "I was just thinking."

"About?" Renee asked, as she hopped back up onto her chair and picked up the salad tongs.

Before Penelope could offer an answer, Zoe skipped into the kitchen. "Mommy? Why were you shouting? Can Alexa and I have cookies?"

Renee turned to her raven haired daughter. "I wasn't really shouting, I was whooping with excitement because Auntie Kris is going to be my work partner."

Zoe beamed at Kris, her smile close to taking over her entire face. "That sounds like fun! Will you be here, more?"

Kris grinned at her niece. "Probably. Is that okay?"

"Yes!" Zoe enthused and did a little dance of joy. "Will you bring Kevin, too?"

"Oh, I don't think so, Sweetie," Renee cut in. "We'll be working during school hours."

Zoe looked thoughtful and then shrugged her slim shoulders. "Okay. Can we have cookies?"

Penelope smiled. Gotta love children. Everything clear and easy, black and white.

Renee hopped off of her chair, pulled a blue, plastic plate from the cupboard and loaded it up with chocolate chip cookies from a jar shaped as a large, pink bunny rabbit. "Can you carry these without spilling? Otherwise, Poppy will eat them as soon as they hit the floor."

Zoe nodded and reached for the blue plate, just as Poppy came scampering through the kitchen doorway. "Oh, no," Zoe admonished, sounding like a miniature version of her mother. "None for you. Chocolate is bad for dogs."

Poppy wagged her tail eagerly and trailed after Zoe as she placed one foot steadily in front of the other, marching with methodical steps out of the kitchen.

Renee shook her head, amused at the picture of her daughter and dog. "So, where were we? Pen, you were saying something, right?"

"No, it's fine."

Renee pulled more cookies from her jar and placed them on a plate on the table. When Kris cocked an eyebrow at the plate, Renee shrugged. "Fiber."

Kris laughed.

"So," Renee encouraged Penelope. "Go ahead, what was it?"

"Well, um," Penelope hesitated, feeling transparent as hell. "Since Kris is going to partner up with you, does that mean she'll take over for me on the, umm ... current project?"

Renee lifted her eyebrows. She knew fully well what Penelope was thinking. Kris, on the other hand wasn't completely up to speed, so, she didn't catch on. Renee stalled for time by taking a long sip from her coffee cup.

"What?" Kris asked, looking back and forth between the two women. "What's with the looks? It's no big deal. Pen can stay on the current project and I'll start up once it's all wrapped up. I don't want to shove my way in."

Renee continued to sip her coffee and stare at Penelope.

"Unless," Kris said, oblivious to the nature of the unspoken words flying between Renee and Penelope. "You're too busy with work and don't have the time, Pen. Then, I'll get right on board."

Penelope put her salad fork on the edge of her plate, reached for a cookie and shrugged, not sure how to reply.

Kris cocked her head. "What's the project, again? It was a whole load of cakes, right?"

"Right," Renee offered.

Kris snapped her fingers and her eyes brightened as, finally, she clued in. "Ooooh, *right*. That's why you're being so quiet. Now I remember."

Penelope exhaled in exasperation. "Don't give me the big-eyed, '*ooooh*', look, okay? It's no big deal --"

"You lie," Renee stated, firmly. "It is a big deal. A huge deal."

Penelope snapped her mouth shut.

Kris looked back and forth between them, a startled expression on her face. "What's going on?"

"What's going on is," Renee practically spat. "It's gone way past the project and infected her personal head space."

Kris' eyes became even wider as she watched Renee sit back, cross her arms and wait for Penelope's response.

"For goodness sake!" Penelope unhinged her jaw and blurted. "You make it sound like I have a disease!"

"A lust disease," Kris commented, nodding her head in an annoyingly knowing manner. "That's the worst kind."

"Get off it!" Penelope protested and dropped her half eaten cookie onto her plate. "It's fine, Scott and I are just friends --"

"Hardly!" Renee volleyed.

Penelope sat up straight in her chair and glared at Renee.

"The only reason its stayed that way is because some sort of ... I don't know, decency, has kept you from letting it take its natural course." Renee pointed her index finger accusingly at Penelope. "Admit it, if you weren't engaged to Ben, we wouldn't even be having this conversation. The deed would have been long done."

"Whoa," Kris looked at Penelope in shock. "Where the hell have I been? How long was I sick? Is that true, Pen? Do you actually think seriously that, if you didn't have Ben, you'd want to, *you know*, with this guy?"

Penelope crossed her arms in front of her chest defensively. "Oh, and you've never thought that about any other man, since you've been with Grayson?"

Kris sat back, first surprised by the question, then thoughtful. "Truthfully? No." She saw the look of disbelief cross Penelope's face and amended. "Not *real* men, men I actually know. Maybe the occasional movie star, but, they're like fictional people and that's never going to happen. They don't really count."

Renee was nodding and Penelope frowned. "You're agreeing? It's the same for you? No one, not one man other than Paul?"

Renee, sighed, placed her salad fork onto her plate and tried to keep the pity out of her voice. "No, Pen. That's what I've been trying to tell you." She spoke softly, trying to cushion her words. "Yes, we might think some celebrity is hot, but, as Kris said, that's not real, it's just silly, girlie stuff."

Kris popped a tomato into her mouth and nodded.

Renee continued. "But, when it comes to actual men we've met in the flesh, we don't think of them in that way. Doesn't matter how cute, or whatever. We think sexually of our husbands, and that's it."

Penelope looked from Renee to Kris, and back, again. They were both wearing an expression of apology, mixed with pity. Penelope swallowed against a lump that had formed in her throat.

"So," she finally said, folding her arms tightly across her chest. "I'm the bad guy, then?"

"What's that supposed to mean?" Renee asked.

"It means, because I'm feeling this whole, so called, '*lust disease*', for the first time ever, I'm a terrible person?"

Kris held up her hand and frowned. "Hold on. What are you saying? You've never really felt like that before? Really, never? But, what about Ben --"

Penelope shook her head. "No! With Ben, it developed differently. He was my friend first, you know that, you introduced us. We evolved from that, instead of that initial, stomach flipping, head-turning stuff."

Kris nodded, encouraging Penelope to continue.

"I mean, sure," Penelope admitted. "I've had crushes on guys, before I met Ben, but, this, well, this feeling of being all jumpy and out of sorts when I see Scott, is a whole other animal."

Kris was speechless. She'd just assumed that Penelope and Ben ... Clearly, she'd assumed incorrectly.

Renee jumped in and attempted to smooth things over. "Listen, you're confused, you haven't done anything drastic, you've done nothing wrong."

Kris wiped the worried look from her face and nodded earnestly. "Renee's right, Pen. Just don't do anything drastic, not until you've had a chance to really think."

Renee reached out to pat Penelope's hand and held out the cookie plate. Penelope grabbed two.

"I don't know," she said, taking a bite and, then, talking around a mouthful of chocolate. "I've never been thrown off balance like this before. I want to get a grip on it, I do. But, then, when I see him ... What if the truth is that this is something like cheating."

"That's ridiculous!" Kris shook her head firmly. "You haven't even so much as hugged the guy!" She picked up her coffee cup and dared to say the next thing on her mind. "You know, maybe Renee's right and you should step back and I'll step in."

"No!" Penelope blurted and Kris jerked, taken aback by her vehemence. "What I mean is," she amended. "I think it's better if I just deal with it. Not run away. Before I move anything along further with Ben."

Kris looked skeptical, and Renee just looked worried, so Penelope blazed forward. "I'm thinking of Ben --"

"Really?" Kris couldn't help herself. She honestly didn't think Ben was even in the equation.

"Yes," Penelope insisted. "Otherwise, it could be one of those terrible 'what-if' sort of situations and that's not good. Not when we're planning to get married."

"Dumb idea," Renee said, bluntly.

"Pardon?" Penelope said, nonplussed.

"I think that is the worst thing you can do," Renee stated, matter-of-fact. "You need to stop having anything to do with this guy, immediately. Or, you're going to do something that you can't step back from."

Penelope felt the hair on the back of her neck rise, like a cat, at the absolute conviction in Renee's voice. "You don't know that," she said, levelly.

"Yes, I do know it, Pen," Renee said, looking her square in the eye. "I'd bet money on it."

Penelope had had enough. She brushed her hands together over her plate and stood up. "Okay, well, you're entitled to your thoughts, even if they're wrong -
-"

"They're not."

Kris slapped Renee on the arm. "Stop!" She said. "Quite making it worse."

Renee refused. "Worse how?" She challenged. "Penelope is playing a dangerous game, pretending she can be friends with this guy, when she really wants to jump him. It's stupid and irresponsible and I'm saying it."

"I'm leaving," Penelope strode across the kitchen.

"I didn't say you were stupid," Renee clarified. "You know that right? I just said the choices that you are making are not ... Very smart."

Penelope rolled her eyes.

"Can we just all calm down for a minute?" Kris said, attempting to pat things down.

"Sure," Penelope nodded. "You two go right ahead. Be calm and collected and happily married, finish your salads and I'll take off and leave you to it."

Before Kris could utter another word, Penelope pulled open the door and was gone.

Penelope pulled into her parking space at work and cut the engine on her car. She was still angry at Renee and, then, even more irritated that she had allowed herself to get angry.

Irresponsible, she silently fumed, how absurd. Renee didn't have any idea what she was talking about. In fact, Penelope had the sudden thought, I'll show her just how responsible I can be.

She pulled out her cell phone and began a text to Scott. It read: "Hi! Sorry cut u off yesterday. Short notice, but, R U free 2nite for dinner?"

Penelope hit send and waited. Please let him hear his phone, she silently prayed. A moment later, her phone buzzed. A new text.

"Hi!" It read. "Yes, dinner sounds great! 7:30 @ Chianti's?"

With trembling fingers, Penelope replied, "Sounds perfect! C U at 7:30!"

She took a breath and started another text, to Ben. "Hi, working late, won't be home for dinner. Make yourself something and see you later." She hit send and dropped her phone back into her bag.

Pretending to be friends, Penelope fumed, hearing Renee's words in her ears. Please. She and Scott didn't have to pretend. They were friends. Besides, what would Renee remember about being a friend to a man? Nothing. The woman had been married for almost ten years, she had lost touch.

The travel agent, her name tag said, 'Sara' in bold letters, smiled at Ben. Ben, sitting in the chair on the other side of her desk, beamed back. Sara wanted to reach out and hug him, for giving her day a pocket of fun. So many people booked their travel tickets on-line, or over the phone, she was finding it thrilling to have an actual customer, in person, while she made up his package.

"So," Sara confirmed. "That's two, round trip, first class tickets to London, England, correct?"

Ben, sitting on the edge of his seat, nodded enthusiastically. "Perfect! It's all perfect. She's going to be so surprised, I can't tell you."

Sara grinned and tucked her blonde hair behind her ears. "She's a lucky woman," she stated. "What a great surprise."

A second travel agent poked her head around the cubicle. Her name tag said, 'Angela', in the same bold type. "Did you say surprise?"

Ben looked up, surprised, and she giggled.

"Sorry, I couldn't help it. I know I shouldn't be listening in, but, I love it when we help organize surprise travel."

Ben laughed and Angela sighed. Too bad, she thought. The good ones were always taken. "So, now that I've gone and done the big, 'no, no,'" she said, saucily. "Where are you taking the mystery woman?"

Ben didn't hesitate. "London! And, the mystery woman is my fiancée."

"Nice," Angela nodded.

Ben took a breath. He couldn't keep it quiet another moment and figured that the odds of these two women telling Penelope were as good as nil. "Not only that, I'm going to suggest we actually get married there!"

The two women looked delighted, and Sara clapped her hands. "Congratulations! God, I envy her," she gushed and, then, caught herself. It wouldn't do for the customer to feel that she was panting over him.

Ben, caught up in his revelation, didn't even notice. "Well, we've been engaged for a while now and I decided that the best thing to do was to put things in motion. Show her how much I want to take that next step and tie the knot."

Angela stared at Ben in amazement. "Wow. You are a rarity? Do you have any brothers?"

"Yes," Ben replied and then quickly amended, when both Angela and Sara visibly perked up. "However, sorry to say, they're both married."

"Of course they are," Sara lamented and shook her head. "All the good ones are."

"I know," Angela threw in. "Where are the decent guys who are still single?"

Ben swallowed, unsure as to whether or not they were just bitching, or actually looking for a reply.

"Anyway," Angela fluffed her long, brown hair. "You don't need us whining on, spoiling your moment." She grinned and walked back to her cubicle, throwing a last comment over her shoulder. "You keep us believing that there's still hope!"

Sara giggled and turned back to Ben. "Okay, now that we have the flights, let's get cracking on your accommodations!"

Ben nodded and sat forward to peruse the brochures that Sara had laid out on her desk.

Penelope checked her cell phone for a reply from Ben. Nothing. She hoped that he had seen her text. She glanced over to where Scott was standing, waiting for their table, and felt her stomach flip, just looking at him. She checked her phone one more time and, still, found nothing.

"Ready?" Scott gently laid a hand on Penelope's shoulder, startling her. She dropped her phone into her bag and turned to him with a smile.

"Yup. All set."

"Excellent," he spoke close to Penelope's ear. "Because, our table is ready."

Penelope smiled at the waiting hostess and suppressed a giggle. The woman had been doing her best to keep her eyes on Penelope, but, there was no question that she had been caught appraising Scott.

Penelope stood tall and proud, amused by the woman's blatant admiration. That's right, she thought, not even flinching as Scott placed a proprietary hand on her lower back. I'm with him.

"Beer?" Grayson asked, as he opened his fridge.

"Sure," Ben replied. "Thanks." He was at Grayson's house, hanging out in the games room, having gone over after receiving Penelope's short message.

"So," Grayson said as he handed Ben his beer and took the seat opposite his brother on the brown leather couch. "Pen didn't say when she'd be home?"

Ben took a long swallow from his bottle, loosened his tie and shook his head. "No." He stopped short as Kris entered the room carrying a large platter of chicken wings and celery.

"Thanks, Hon," Grayson said. They were back on solid ground since Kris had finally admitted that she was ready to stop fussing and do what she really wanted, work with Renee. "Did you say that you'd seen Pen today?"

Ben sat forward and Kris felt a wash of guilt overtake her. She hated this. "Sure, at Renee's, at lunch." She averted her eyes from Ben and focused upon placing the platter on the coffee table.

"That's probably why she's going to be late, then," Grayson offered as he reached for a wing.

Ben sighed, placed his beer on the table and sunk back into the couch. "Yeah, you're probably right. I'm making a big deal out of nothing. She was just so abrupt in her message ... I don't know."

"Gray's probably right," Kris said, reaching for the remote to turn down the volume on the TV. She couldn't stand Ben being so worried and wanted to soothe him. "We did chat for a while at lunch and she did say she had a lot of work waiting at the office, before she left."

Ben looked thoughtful and Grayson nodded at Kris. "Makes sense to me," he said, chicken wing poised at his mouth.

"I suppose," Ben shrugged. "But ..."

Grayson paused and looked at his brother. "What?"

Kris's eyes widened. Shit.

"I don't know," Ben said. "She seems okay, she did her makeover thing and seems happy with that, but, then there have been some times, when she doesn't realize I'm watching, that she gets this *look* on her face -
-"

"What do you mean, *look*?" Grayson asked, then took a bite out of his chicken wing.

Against her better judgment, Kris froze. She would rather have run from the room, but, under the circumstances, thought it might look a tad bit suspicious.

"Like she's off someplace else, in her head. Like she's with me, but, then, not with me." Ben exhaled in exasperation. "Do you get what I mean? Has Kris ever had that sort of look?"

Kris, still frozen, felt her pulse accelerate. How did she get dragged into it?

Grayson chewed and looked thoughtful. Finally, he nodded. "Yeah, I suppose I know what you mean."

Ben felt relieved and reached for his beer.

"But," Grayson added, as he dropped the bones from his wing onto the side of the plate. "I've never thought anything of it. I've never taken it personally against me. She has a lot of stuff on her plate, on a daily basis, so, it only makes sense that she'd have to take moments here and there to go off in her head to sort through it."

Kris slowly released the breath she had been holding. She wanted nothing more than to slap Ben. Her pity was gone and, in it's place, was annoyance.

Whatever his troubles were with Penelope, he didn't have to come in and start creating waves in her house!

"Did you ever think that it might be the same for Pen?" Grayson asked. "She does a lot of stuff, too. Her being distracted doesn't immediately mean that she's doing, or thinking, something suspicious."

"Yeah, I know," Ben reluctantly agreed, as he placed his beer bottle on a coaster. He didn't think that he would be able to find the words, anyway, that could express the mixed, back and forth, vibe he had been getting from Penelope. It was just a gut feeling he had, that she was more than just busy, but, how to explain *that*, without sounding paranoid, he didn't know.

"Distraction can just be distraction," Grayson stated, while wiping his fingers on a paper napkin.

"You're probably right," Ben said and reached for a chicken wing.

Grayson grinned. "Sometimes, it's better to just let things be. Over thinking it can make something, out of a whole lot of nothing."

Kris slipped out of the room, finally, as the two men moved their conversation onto sports. She tiptoed upstairs to the kitchen and began to wipe down her gleaming counter tops, her churning thoughts making her too restless to sit.

Renee was completely on the mark, Penelope was playing a dangerous game. Kris genuinely hoped that she would get it all straightened out before it was too late, someone got hurt, or, a step was taken that couldn't be taken back.

"Whew," Penelope exhaled as she stepped out of the restaurant into the cool, night air. "That feels good."

Scott, in step beside her, nodded.

Penelope placed one heeled foot in front of the other and stumbled a bit as she walked. Maybe she'd had one glass of wine too many.

"Whoa," Scott grinned and reached for her arm. "Watch your step, there."

Penelope giggled. Okay, she definitely felt light headed. She hadn't noticed it when she was sitting down at their table, but, outside in the parking lot, she was seriously tipsy.

They arrived to stand by her car and Penelope breathed deeply, in an attempt to clear her head. It wasn't working.

"Don't take this the wrong way," Scott offered, standing close enough that Penelope could feel the heat of his breath on her skin. "But, I don't think that you should be driving."

"I agree!" She declared, and then started giggling, again, as she wobbled on her heels.

Scott chuckled and slipped an arm around her waist.

Mmm, nice, Penelope thought and inhaled his musky scent.

"I can take you home, if you like --"

"My car," Penelope gestured to her red Eclipse. "I can't leave it here."

"No problem," Scott assured her. "I'll talk to the manager, tell him what we're doing and you can get your car tomorrow."

Penelope grinned. "That sounds like a good plan. You know, for such a hottie, you're pretty smart."

Scott threw his head back and laughed.

Penelope slapped a hand across her mouth, shocked that she'd spoken her thoughts out loud.

"Okay," Scott said, still grinning. "Let's get to my car and get you off of your feet."

"You're a good friend," Penelope said and leaned into him. "Everyone thinks that they know so much, but, you're my friend, right?"

Scott looked down at her, his eyes dark and thoughtful. "What is everyone saying, exactly?"

Penelope blinked a few times to get her focus. "They think that we're more than friends, but, I've told them that you don't think that way. Right?"

Scott went silent as he looked at her. He placed his both his hands on her waist and gently turned her to face him, then reached a hand to her chin and tipped her face upward. Penelope knew what was coming and ... she waited.

Scott inclined his head and met her lips with his own, giving her a kiss so sweet, so full of heat and desire, that, had he not had a hold of her, she would have fallen off of her heels.

When they came up for air, Scott met her eyes with his own and said, "What do you think?"

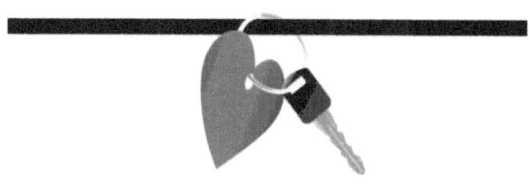

Nine

Penelope poured herself a cup of coffee and shook two pain pills from their container, into the palm of her hand. Even that sound was too loud for her aching head. She swallowed the tablets, balking slightly at the heat of the coffee, and massaged her temple with her free hand. What the hell she had been thinking, drinking so much wine? She never drank that much and she could only imagine what Scott must have thought ...

Oh, God, Scott.

Penelope slipped into a chair at the kitchen table, put down her cup and dropped her head into her hands. Jesus, she thought. Never mind the wine, what had she been thinking, letting him kiss her like that?

After that kiss, the rest of the evening was a bit hazy. She knew that Scott had driven her home, well, okay, a couple of doors down in case Ben had seen her arrive, and then she'd stumbled into the house, all ready to blather about her lateness, and she'd found ... silence.

Ben had already gone up to bed and she had been spared the humiliation of a drunken confession. Sitting in her kitchen, in the light of day, Penelope wondered if it was a second chance to stop things in their tracks, or a nail biting agony until she couldn't stop herself from blurting the truth.

But, that kiss ... Wow. Even with her head aching and her conscience wincing, Penelope had to admit that that kiss was ...

"Morning."

"Good God!" Penelope exclaimed, and then grimaced as she whirled around to face Ben.

"Sorry," Ben yawned and rubbed at the blonde stubble on his chin. "I thought you heard me."

"No," Penelope shook her head, carefully. "I didn't."

Ben watched her and Penelope averted her eyes from his direct stare. There was a note in his voice. A tone that alerted her to the fact that he seemed to be aware that something was amiss. She stood up and busied herself, pouring cream into her cup.

"Coffee?" She asked, keeping her eyes on the cream container.

"Thanks," Ben replied, his gaze steady. "So, tell me, when did you get home? I didn't hear you come in."

Penelope turned her back on him to reach into the cupboard for another cup and spoke over her shoulder. "Oh, I'm not sure, exactly." She placed the cup on the counter top and picked up the carafe.

Ben waited.

"When I got home, you were already asleep," she filled the cup. "So, I didn't want to wake you --"

Ben reached for his coffee and continued to wait, saying nothing. Penelope wasn't sure what to make of it and was growing increasingly agitated.

"That's it?" he said, his voice flat. "That's all you've got to say?"

Penelope stiffened. His tone was definitely accusatory. "What? What else do you want me to say?"

Ben raised an eyebrow. "You aren't going to say anything at all about the fact that you chose not to sleep in our bed?"

Penelope flinched at the brittleness in his voice and then guilt hit her in a wave so forceful, she took the defense. "What? What's the big deal? You've slept on the couch, many times, and you haven't heard me giving you grief about it."

Ben shook his head. "Unbelievable."

Penelope strode across the room, away from him, into the family room. He was too close for comfort. She gritted her teeth. "Are you even talking to me, or just yourself?"

Ben turned and faced her square on. "I think I could probably say the exact same thing to you!"

Penelope crossed her arms over her chest. "What are we even talking about, Ben? Because, you're making no sense. I came in late, didn't want to wake you, so I slept in the guest room. That's it. All because I was thinking of you!"

Ben nodded, his face stiff, and placed his coffee cup beside hers, on the table.

Penelope huffed, draping herself in indignation at having to explain. "I don't even get what your problem is!"

"Really? Well, let me tell you my *problem*, as you so kindly put it." Ben fired back. "I think that something is going on with you. I don't know what it is, but it's something. And," he put up a hand to silence her. "*And*, I think that it's time you came clean with me, or, I don't know what the hell we're even doing!"

Penelope recoiled as though she'd been slapped. She looked at Ben, his eyes flashing with hurt and anger, his posture strong and poised, and couldn't help but think that it was a side of him she had never before seen. A passionate side. A committed side. It was so off the mark of how she thought of him that it confused her. She felt light headed, and slightly nauseous from all of the wine.

Ben watched the emotions as they flitted across Penelope's face. He knew that there was something that she wasn't saying and, while he knew it might not turn out to be what he wanted to hear, he was willing to take that chance. Anything was better than living in limbo.

"Well?" He pushed. "Are you coming clean with me, or not?"

Penelope bit her lower lip, determined not to cry. She was too tired and, truth be told, too hung over, to deal with what was happening. Like a child, she wanted to run away. "Fine," she spat. "I don't know, okay? I don't know what I'm thinking, or feeling, about any of it! I want something, I know that I do, except I'm not even sure where, or *who*, I want it from."

Ben frowned. She wasn't being clear. "Whoa," he shook his head, registering her last words. "*Who*? What are you saying --"

"Basically," she cut him off. "It's all a mixed up jumble and, for now, that's going to have to do!" She pushed past him and walked toward the staircase. "I know I've more or less said nothing, but, how can I tell you something that I don't even know?"

Ben watched as she bolted up the stairs and exhaled the breath he'd been holding. What a mess. Penelope had made no discernible sense and he was feeling more confused, instead of less. He was at a loss as to what to do, but, yet, felt he had to do something. After all, anything had to be better than nothing, right?

"Hey, Pen," Renee's voice trilled through Penelope's cell phone headset.

"Hi, what's up?" She responded as she made a left turn into the mall parking lot and then waited patiently for an elderly man to pull out of his parking space.

"I have great news!"

Penelope swung into the vacated space and turned off the car. "Excellent, I could use some."

"What's wrong?" Renee asked, picking up immediately on the flatness in Penelope's tone.

"Nothing, I'm fine."

"Really?"

"Yes, just a little tired. I had a tiff with Ben, then, had to get a cab to get my car ... It's nothing."

"Your car? What happened to your car?"

Oh, hell, Penelope thought. Why did she have to go and say that?

"Pen?"

"Nothing, the car is fine, everything is fine."

"Okay," Renee hesitated. "If you're sure ..."

"I'm sure."

"Because, if you're trying to spare my feelings and you're secretly still mad at me about what I said yesterday --"

"No, I'm not," Penelope assured her. "You were just looking out for me, I get that."

"Oh, thank goodness," Renee said, the relief in her voice palpable. "I'm so glad that you understand that. I'll always look out for you."

"And, me, for you," Penelope told her as she let her sore head flop back against the car's headrest. Good God, she was tired. "Now, tell me, what's this great news?"

"Right!" Renee happily refocused. "I have all of the information I need on the architect cake project, so, you're free of it! I spoke to the head guy, well, one of the head guys, yesterday, after you left, and he told me that nothing else is going to change, so, that's it."

Penelope sat up straight. "Okay, so, I guess that means --"

"Yup, that means you don't need to arrange any more meetings with Scott, or anyone else who works there." Renee added the last part out of kindness, knowing full well that Penelope had not met with anyone other than Scott.

"Okay," Penelope said, again, realizing that she was using that word an awful lot. "But, if you need anything else --"

"Of course!" Renee assured, her voice slightly shrill. "But, I don't. And, I doubt I will. So, you can just stop seeing Scott. Stop seeing him and let him live his life. Live his life in any way that he sees fit."

Penelope frowned. "Ren, I think it's my turn to ask, are you okay?"

"Me?" Renee chirped. "Sure! Why wouldn't I be? I'm perfect and I'll be even more perfect when you just turn away from that Single Dad guy and go back to your own stuff."

It was the "that Single Dad guy" comment that did it for Penelope. "What's going on, Ren? What aren't you telling me?"

"Nothing! I'm telling you nothing!"

"Well, *that's* obvious --"

"No, that's not how I meant it!" Renee stumbled over her words. "I'm just saying that there's nothing *new* to tell, nothing new at all."

"Okay," Penelope stated. "Either you spit it out right this minute, or I'm coming over there and stand on your doorstep until you do." She was hit by a flash of inspiration. "*Or*, I'll call Kris and ask her what's going on!"

"No!" Renee blurted and Penelope nodded. She knew that would work. "Okay, I'll tell you, but, you have to promise not to get all wonky over it."

"I cannot promise you anything, when I don't know what it is, can I?"

Renee sighed. "Fine. But, just remember, don't shoot the messenger." She took a deep breath and plunged forward. "Kris found out something about Single Dad. Something, um, not-so-nice about him."

Penelope concentrated on her breathing, taking it all in. "Okay, what did she find out?"

"Apparently, he's a bit of a womanizer. And," Renee added. "Before you jump in and say that that sounds like gossip, she received the information from a very good source."

Penelope frowned. "Who?"

"Another Mom, from the school --"

"Oh, well, then, that settles it. The Mom hotline."

"Pen," Renee warned. "You asked, so I'm telling."

"Fine."

Renee nodded, even though Penelope couldn't see her over the phone, and continued. "There's another Mom, who is good friends with a divorced Mom, and she said that the divorced Mom was talking very fondly of Scott and his *abilities*."

"Abilities?" Penelope sat up straight in her seat.

Renee coughed uncomfortably and cleared her throat. "And, apparently, that divorced Mom said that he is dating yet another newly divorced woman, helping her through her time of adjustment. It's sort of his thing, if you will. Something he's getting a bit of a reputation for."

Penelope felt her cheeks go hot at the very idea of Scott, his *abilities* and another, faceless, woman.

"Hello? Pen, are you still there?"

Penelope swallowed against the rise of nausea that had risen in her throat. "Yes, I'm still here. I'm just digesting what you said."

"I'm really sorry to have to be the one to tell you," Renee apologized.

"Well, it is just a rumor --"

"No," Renee insisted. "No, it's not. It's the truth."

"Were you there?" Penelope asked, starting to get angry. "Did you actually see Scott comforting this mystery woman?"

"Oh, *Pen*," Renee groaned.

"No, really, were you?" Penelope was working herself up into a serious lather. "Because, if you weren't, then it is still hearsay. And," she slapped her steering wheel for emphasis. "I'll do everyone a favor and get to the bottom of this, so we can clear up the rumor. When I next talk to Scott, I'll ask him if what you've said is true!"

"Okay, okay," Renee said, wishing she had a white flag to wave. "I'm sorry I said anything. But, the rest of what I said, about not needing any more information for the cakes, is actually the truth. I spoke to the guy at the firm personally. No second hand information, no hearsay, or rumors."

"Good." Penelope stated. "Well, I'm glad I could help, but, I need to go now."

"Okay," Renee said. "I won't keep you."

"Bye." Penelope pressed the end button on her cell phone and massaged the bridge of her nose. A tiny, nagging voice in her head was insisting that she listen to reason and she wanted nothing more than to shut it up. She needed noise and chaos for distraction, not to mention some serious carbs to settle her stomach. The mall was calling as her salvation.

Ben turned off his computer and stretched his arms above his head. He hadn't heard a word out of Penelope all day and it was making him nutty. He picked up his cell phone and dialed her number, crossing his fingers that when she saw his number, she'd actually pick up.

"Hello?"

Ben sat up straight in his chair. "Pen? It's me."

"Yeah, I know. I saw your name on the call display."

"Listen," he said. "I'm sorry about this morning ..."

"It's fine," she cut him off. "Forget about it."

"Where are you?" Ben asked. He could hear noise in the background and couldn't place it.

"At the mall." Penelope cleared her throat. "I've been here pretty much all day. A bit of retail therapy and all that."

Ben grinned. A joke, that was a good sign. "Are you coming home?"

Penelope hesitated a fraction of a second before answering. Was she? "I guess so. I mean, it is getting late --"

"Listen," Ben cut in. "I was thinking. Why don't we have a date? You know, go to a movie, then get some dinner and talk. We haven't done that in a long time and I think we need it."

Penelope sighed and nodded. He was right. She had had her time to think and it was imperative that she shared her thoughts and feelings. She couldn't keep them a secret any longer, he deserved to know that she wanted to run away with another man. "Okay, that sounds like a good idea. It's a date."

Ben exhaled, suddenly aware that he had been holding his breath, waiting for her reply. "Excellent. Do you want to come home first, or just meet?"

"Ummm--"

"Or, wait! Even better! I'll quickly get myself together and clear out, and then you can come home, freshen up and we'll set a time and place to meet."

Penelope closed her eyes, trying to block out the guilt swimming in her vision. He was so nice, so decent, it was painful. "Okay, that sounds great," she said, her voice thick with suppressed emotion. "Thank you."

"Of course, Sweetie," Ben said, gently. "For you, anything."

"I have to go now," Penelope sniffed. "I'll head home in about half an hour, okay?"

"I'll be gone," Ben stated. "I'll leave a note to let you know where we can meet and at what time."

"Okay," Penelope agreed and hung up. She took a deep, shaky breath and rolled her shoulders. She had to do it. It was the decent thing to do. And, the one thing that Ben deserved was her decency.

Ben leaned casually against a pillar near the entrance to the movie theatre. He checked his watch and then scanned the crowd for Penelope. They had about a half hour until their show started, but, still, he was a little worried that she might change her mind and just not show up at all.

A flash of bright, auburn hair caught his eye and Ben moved slightly to his left, to look around a couple standing in his sight line. He felt his breath catch as Penelope came into view. She looked beautiful in her red trench coat, a pair of dark wash jeans and leopard print, platform heels. Ben was amazed that, after so much time, just the sight of her could make his heart beat faster. He resolved, right then and there, that he would do anything in his power to remind her of their connection. He would be patient, he would be forgiving, he would love her.

She hadn't spotted him, so, Ben was free to watch her, and enjoy the view, as she walked toward the theater. Suddenly, she glanced his way and he plastered a smile on his face while raising a hand in greeting. She smiled back and threaded her way through the crowd to arrive at his side.

"Hi!" Ben enthused, doing his best to seem positive, as opposed to nervous as hell.

Penelope leaned in to hug him. "Sorry, I'm late."

"No," Ben inhaled her scent. "No, you're right on time. I was a bit early, but, figured I'd just hang around and people watch."

Penelope grinned, trying to keep things light, and followed his lead. "Anything interesting?"

He moved closer, lowered his voice and spoke near her ear. "Actually, I've been getting a bit of a show from a couple to my right. I'm hoping that, if they're going to the same movie as us, they sit in the back. Otherwise, we'll be way too distracted to watch the screen."

Penelope nodded and casually shifted her weight from one foot to the other, trying not to be obvious, to get a better look at the couple. She glanced over, and then caught her breath as her knees went weak.

"Pen?" Ben said, his voice concerned as Penelope's face drained of color.

Penelope ignored him and kept on staring. The man and woman were just finishing a deep, passionate kiss and, as the man came up for air, he glanced to his right, making direct eye contact with Penelope. It was Scott.

Penelope turned sharply to face Ben, but, not before seeing the wide-eyed, startled look on Scott's face. She wanted to run away, far away, where no on, especially not Scott, could see her. However, as Ben was looking at her with genuine concern, Penelope knew that she had to get a grip on herself, and quickly.

"Jeez, you're really white. Are you okay?" Ben asked, his face a mask of worry. "Are you not feeling well? Do we need to leave?"

Penelope started to nod, thinking that faking illness was the perfect excuse, when she heard Scott's deep voice directly behind her.

"Penelope?"

Penelope swallowed and bit her lip as she tried to keep a hold of her emotions. She plastered, what she hoped was, a surprised look upon her face and turned around. "Scott! Hi! How are you?"

Ben pulled his shoulders back and watched the scene before him. It was obvious that the guy knew Penelope and, judging from her reaction, it wasn't casually. The woman hanging off of the guy's arm seemed a bit out of place, but, then, watching Penelope, Ben figured that he, too, probably looked much the same as the woman.

Scott gestured to the woman on his arm. "This is Tamara."

Tamara smiled and nodded as she checked her lip line with her finger for traces of smudged lip gloss. Penelope wanted to smack her.

Scott waited a beat and looked pointedly at Ben.

"Hi," Ben said, reaching across Penelope. "I'm Ben."

"Oh, excuse me," Penelope said, still feeling light headed. "Sorry. Ben, this is Scott, a client of Renee's. And, of course, *Tammy --*"

"Tamara," Scott corrected and, then, seeing the expression upon Penelope's face, wished he hadn't.

"And, this is Ben, my fiancé." Penelope finished, her face set like stone.

"Oh, how nice!" Tamara gushed, finished with her lip inspection. She squeezed Scott's arm in a proprietary manner and Penelope's nostrils flared with annoyance. "When are you getting married?"

Ben was completely distracted by the conversation not being said, between Penelope and Scott. Tamara's words barely made it to his ears. He gave his head a light shake and tried to be polite. "Oh, well, you know, we haven't exactly fixed a date, yet."

Penelope nodded stiffly. She needed to get away from Scott and his chippy, and she needed to do it immediately.

"Should we get our seats?" she said, abruptly, to Ben, not caring if she was rude. "We should, I think. Don't want to miss our show." She turned her back on Scott and looked up at Ben expectantly.

"Right!" Ben quickly picked up her cue. "Well, nice meeting you."

He turned his head from Scott to Tamara, but, made eye contact with neither. Scott was watching the back of Penelope's head, while Tamara was leaning into Scott, staring rapturously up at him. Wow. Ben walked swiftly beside Penelope, barely able to keep up with her fast strides toward the theatre.

Penelope sat ramrod straight in her seat and concentrated upon her breathing. She absolutely could not break down in front of Ben. Even though Renee had told her about Scott, she hadn't believed it for a moment and, now ... She was filled with so many emotions, most of them wrapped in hurt and confusion that, if she allowed even a crack in her resolve, she feared she'd start howling and be unable to stop.

Ben sat in the seat beside Penelope, his thoughts going a mile a minute. He was trying to put together what had just happened. Penelope's mood had shifted so rapidly, in such a short space of time, it didn't take a whole lot of brains to figure out that it was connected to that guy. That client. But how?

Ben shifted in his seat and watched Penelope, out of the corner of his eye. She was upset. Visibly so. What had that guy done to get her worked up? Had he been rude? Or, dismissive? Or, worse yet, flirtatious? Ben, ran his fingers through his short, blonde hair and wished his thoughts would shut up. He had a strong feeling that, if he probed any deeper, he'd be sorry that he did.

"I think I need some air," Penelope said, and abruptly stood up.

Ben, startled from his reverie, nodded and also stood, making room for Penelope to pass.

"I'll be back in a sec," she said and walked swiftly up the theater aisle.

Ben watched her go and just as he was about to sit back down, a large movement from the back of the theatre caught his eye. It was Scott. He was stumbling over the people in his aisle, then left the theatre at a brisk pace, following in Penelope's footsteps. Ben didn't even hesitate. There was no way that he was missing whatever was about to transpire between his fiancée and this recently added stranger.

Ben dashed through the theatre doors and frantically scanned the area for any sign of Penelope. A flash of red from her jacket caught his eye and, sure enough, he spotted her, striding across the open area of the theatre lobby, Scott in hot pursuit. He waited a beat, watched them round a concrete pillar, and then hoofed it, to follow their path.

"Penelope, *please*," Ben could hear Scott pleading, as he arrived to stand on the opposite side of the pillar.

The tone was so familiar, so intimate, Ben felt momentarily nauseous. He leaned against the concrete, all pride throw aside as he made the choice to eavesdrop on their conversation. It was the only way he was going to learn anything, about what was happening to his fiancée.

Tucked into the nook, away from prying eyes and ears, Penelope whirled around to face Scott. Her eyes brimmed with tears and she shook her head. "No, Scott, not here. It's too much."

"It's just a date, Penelope," Scott said. "Nothing more." He ran his fingers through his dark hair. "And, to be honest with you, I don't know why we're even having this issue."

Penelope looked at him, incredulous. "Just a date? Nothing more? No big deal? Is that what you're saying?" She didn't let him respond. "So, I've just been imagining everything? This past month, that kiss last night, all my imagination?"

Ben, still standing on the opposite side of the pillar, felt as though he'd been slapped. A month? A kiss? What in the hell was she talking about? Was he sure he wanted to hear this?

"That depends upon what you're saying," Scott countered.

Penelope let out a harsh laugh. "Right. Okay, if I have to spell it out, so be it." She squared her shoulders to face him. "There has definitely been something here, Scott," she pointed back and forth between them. "Yes, at first, it was friendship, but, I'd say that last night, it became something more. And, if you're trying to deny that, then, fine, I can't stop you." She looked him directly in the eye. "But, you'll be a liar and we'll both know it."

Scott broke eye contact and folded his arms across his chest. "Okay, maybe so, but, so what?" He quickly unfolded his arms and pointed at the ring on her left hand. "You've got *that*, so, I'd say that pretty much says it all."

Penelope felt as though her engagement ring had instantly double the weight of her hand. "But, it doesn't," she said. "And, you know it. Otherwise, you wouldn't have gotten involved with me --"

"Involved?" Scott replied, his voice incredulous. "I'd hardly say we've become involved. We've had some meals together, some great conversation, we've had some fun. Hardly the stuff of deep romance --"

"You asshole!" Penelope blurted, her voice thick with unshed tears. "Don't you dare be so terrible as to pass off everything, as though it meant nothing!"

Ben, hearing the passion in Penelope's voice, almost groaned out loud. He felt as though he'd been sucker punched in the stomach. He held his breath a moment, to settle his racing heart, and then leaned in closer. He couldn't go back, he had to know all of it.

Scott's resolve began to slip. He looked at the emotion on Penelope's face and silently cursed. If he had only listened to that small voice in his head the day he had met her ...

"Fine," he nodded, pulling his gaze from her face. "Okay, you're right. It hasn't been nothing, but, still," he gestured to her engagement ring. "That's real, and this isn't."

Penelope was about to protest, but, Scott held up his hand. "Please, hear me out."

Penelope took a deep breath and nodded. "Okay."

Scott leaned against the enclave wall, suddenly tired. "It's pretty simple. You know that my wife died and, as I'm sure you can imagine, a bit of me died with her."

He met Penelope's eyes and then looked at the floor. "All a bit melodramatic, I know, but, there it is."

Penelope hugged herself, feeling torn apart by what he was saying.

"And, I did what so many," he hesitated, then steeled himself to say the word. "*Widowers* do. I closed myself off. I wasn't about to go through that, again."

Penelope resisted the urge to reach out and hug him. She was still angry, but, at the same time, felt a surge of pity.

Scott ran his hand through his dark hair and grinned wryly, despite the shadow of pain that had slipped into his eyes. "And, then, you showed up, Penelope. So different from my wife, but, yet, in so many ways, the same."

Penelope shifted uncomfortably and fidgeted with the belt on her jacket.

"I didn't let myself think about it all that much at first," he sighed. "But, the truth is, after a while I had to face it. When I'm with you, it feels like I'm with a part of her. Like I get to be the Me I was, when I was with her. I'm sorry if that sounds terribly selfish and inconsiderate of you, but, it felt so good, I didn't want to let that go."

"Oh," Penelope said, at a loss for words.

He stopped to swallow against the lump that had formed in his throat and take a breath. "You are the first woman, since my wife died, who has allowed me access to that part of me, again."

Penelope gave him a small smile. "That's a good thing, right?"

Scott nodded, his eyes warm. "Yes, a very good thing. At least I know, no matter how deeply I buried that part of myself, it's still there." He looked at her imploringly. "Can you understand, then, why I felt compelled to pursue you? Even if I come across as a selfish ass?"

Penelope nodded. She understood. In the same circumstances, she might have done the same thing.

Encouraged, Scott continued. "Okay, so, then, you also should understand why I said that this thing, between us, isn't real. But, *that*," he gestured, again, to her ring. "Is very real."

Penelope looked at her ring and ran her thumb across its top.

Scott's face twisted in apology. "Being with you, Penelope, has made me face the fact that I'm still not over my wife. And, I'm so sorry if I made things confusing for you, or hurt you, in any way."

"Oh, well," Penelope shrugged, not sure what to say. Usually, she was the first one with something to say, it was a novelty to be without words.

"I've tried to push it all under the rug, date lots of women, and all that. But, in the end, it was just waiting for me to face it, you know?" He sighed and rubbed at the dark stubble along his jawline. "And, now, I know that I have to. If anything, just to make sure that I don't hurt someone, again, as wonderful and decent as you."

Emotion welled up inside of Penelope and she let out a small sob. She'd been so foolish. She'd let her own illusions and fantasies cloud the reality of what was before her. And, then, there was Ben ... What had she been doing to him?

Scott reached out a tentative hand and touched Penelope's arm. She didn't flinch so he kept it there. "Look, I'm really so sorry --"

"No," Penelope shook her head and wiped the tears that had spilled from her eyes. "I understand, really, I do. It makes sense." She cleared her throat. "But, now, I have to make sense of my stuff. This has been like a huge slap in the face. I feel like I'm seeing clearly for the first time since we met."

Scott squeezed her arm gently and she gave him a small smile.

"You're a force to be reckoned with, Scott, no doubt about it. It's been a real ride, but, I'm ready for something more." She frowned with concern. "I just hope that the man I'm ready for, is still ready for me."

Scott caressed her arm with his thumb. "If he's not, he's a fool, Penelope. A great, big fool. Keep my number, okay, just in case?"

Penelope laughed and let him envelope her in a hug. She inhaled his musky scent and, instead of wanting to sink further into him, she thought of Ben. That had to be something, right?

When things went quiet, Ben, still leaning on the wall around the corner from Penelope and Scott, silently pulled himself away. He walked swiftly to the entrance of the bathrooms and then turned to watch the direction from where Penelope and Scott would emerge. She didn't need to know he'd heard it all. All that mattered was that he did and he could put things right, without any confusion about the real story.

He continued to watch and wait and, a moment later, his patience was rewarded. Penelope and Scott emerged from the nook. They walked separately toward the theatre doors and Ben waited a beat. Just as Penelope was about to go inside, he called out. "Penelope!"

Penelope whirled around and, when she saw Ben, her face broke into a huge grin. He waved and walked from the bathroom entrance toward her. "Good thing I saw you, or we might have been walking around in the dark, trying to find each other."

"Sorry I took so long --"

Ben waved her words away. "It's fine, but, listen, do you really feel like seeing this show?" He tucked his hands into the pockets of his leather jacket to retrieve his keys. "Because, if you don't care, I think I'd rather grab something to eat and go home and talk."

Penelope nodded. "That's the best idea I've heard all day."

Penelope parked her car in its usual spot, beside Ben's, in their garage and pulled her keys out of the ignition. After they had left the movie theater, they had stopped to pick up Chinese food and Penelope knew that Ben was already inside the house, waiting for her.

God, she was nervous! She shook out her hands as she entered the house, hoping to dispel some of her trepidation. She had no idea what was going to come next and felt slightly ill at the thought. It could very well turn out to be their last meal together.

"I'm in here," Ben called out to her, from the kitchen.

The smell of the Chinese food permeated the air and, as Penelope walked into the room, her stomach rumbled. "Can I help?" she ventured, unable to read Ben's mood.

"No, you relax," he pulled chopsticks from a bag and set them on the table. "Do you want plates?"

"Sure, good," Penelope said, feeling like a guest in her own home as she chose her chopsticks, then wondered where she should sit. Finally, she decided to perch on a chair at the table.

Ben reached into a cupboard and took out plates, handing one of them to Penelope. "Dig in while it's all hot."

Penelope did as she was told, serving noodles, rice, chicken and vegetables onto her plate. Even though she was hungry, she didn't know how she was going to get a mouthful past her lips. She felt so tense she thought she might be developing lockjaw.

"Smells good," Ben said as he filled his plate with food.

Penelope nodded, unable to remember a time when she'd been so tongue-tied. If they were going to talk, Ben was going to have to get the ball rolling.

"So," Ben said, around a mouthful of noodles. "I guess we should jump right in, huh?" Before Penelope could respond, he pushed forward. "Things haven't been right for a while, Pen."

"I know," she agreed and tried to eat a small bite of chicken.

"I've been mulling things over for a while now and I think I have some answers."

Penelope looked up from her plate, anxious as to what answers he may have found.

"We can't go on like this. We're really good together, no question, and we have a really nice life, but, still --"

"Ben," Penelope said, her heart beginning to beat faster. "Before you go on --"

"I *know*, Pen." He replied.

Penelope nearly choked on her chicken. "Know?"

"Yes, I know that you've been having second thoughts, about us."

Penelope put her plate down on the table. "Oh, God, Ben, you make it sound so much more --"

"More?"

"More *tragic*, than it is." Penelope got up from her chair and started to pace.

Ben nodded and placed his plate next to Penelope's on the table. "But, it is tragic. Don't you see? I think it's a terrible thing that you would feel second thoughts about me, about us. Especially when I don't. I didn't."

Penelope paused in her pacing. The word "didn't" hung in the air between them. What did it mean? Was he now having second thoughts, because of her issues? Penelope felt, for the second time that evening, that she wanted to howl in frustration. Everything was so mixed up and, yet, finally, she was so very clear about her feelings.

"Ben," she said, desperate to make him understand. "Yes, I was mixed up. But, I'm not anymore."

Ben turned to face her. "What are you saying? I want to hear you say it."

"I'm saying that, yes, I had some moments of confusion. Cold feet, or whatever. And, it did make me question everything. However, it wasn't a bad thing, it was a good thing."

Ben leaned forward in his seat, his face neutral.

Penelope pressed on. "It was a good thing because it helped me to get things really settled in my head and, now, I'm here." She looked around at her house, her home, and felt desperation claw at her breast. She couldn't lose this. Not after she knew the truth of where her heart lay.

She walked over to Ben and dropped to her knees on the floor in front of him. "I'm here now, with you. And, I want this. Us. If you'll have me."

Ben stood up, leaving Penelope still kneeling on the floor. He walked into the family room and stood, facing away from her. She waited, barely breathing. Finally, he turned to face her.

"You know, I thought that this," he swept the air around him with his arm. "Was all I wanted." He walked past her to stand beside the kitchen sink. "Turns out I was wrong. I don't think that this is going to work anymore."

Penelope stood up, shaken and stricken. It was too late. She'd ruined it. "Ben," she pleaded.

"No," Ben shook his head and Penelope fell silent. "Life is about changes, Pen. And, sometimes those changes are scary. But, we can't turn our backs on them, just because they mean going forward into experiences we've never had."

Penelope sank into a chair and clutched at her stomach. What had she done? And, for what?

Ben turned to reach into the top drawer beside the sink and pulled out a folder. Penelope frowned, confused. Was he giving her some sort of divorce papers? They weren't legally married.

Ben walked across the kitchen and held the folder out for Penelope. She didn't want to take it, but, when he stood there, waiting, she reluctantly held out her hand.

Ben nodded and placed the folder into her hand. "I guess what I'm trying to saying is, are you going to go your own way, or, are you willing to change with me?"

Penelope blinked, looked down at the folder, then back up at Ben. "I don't understand."

He gestured to the folder. "Open it."

She took a breath and tentatively pulled it open. Inside the folder were papers, brightly colored and inviting. Alongside the papers, were the tickets that Ben had purchased for his surprise trip to London.

Penelope's eyes widened and she looked up at him, bewildered. "What is this?"

Ben's face broke into a wide grin, his eyes dancing with hope and excitement. "Two tickets, first class, to London, England. The details are all there."

"But," Penelope said, her thoughts scrambled. "I thought ... I was sure ..."

Ben reached out to grab her free hand. "Before we go any further, you have to answer my question."

"Your question?"

"Yes. The one I just asked. Are you willing to change with me?"

Suddenly, everything came into sharp focus for Penelope. Ben wasn't saying he wanted them to go their separate ways, he was saying he wanted them to join together. Thank God. She started to laugh with relief.

"Is that a yes?" Ben asked, mentally crossing his fingers in hope.

"Yes!" Penelope said, giddy with excitement at what lay in her hands. "Yes, I'll change with you!"

"Yes!" Ben whooped as he pulled Penelope out of her chair and into his arms.

She continued to laugh as he kissed her face, and all that he could think was, finally, it was time. They were going to move forward and get on with their lives, together.

Whatever had happened, or not, with that Scott, Ben didn't care. He knew that many other men would insist on details, but, he wasn't other men. He loved Penelope and, what's more, he trusted her. He was absolutely certain that, confused or not, she had continued to hold his heart carefully.

If anything, he had come to the decision that he could spare a tiny thought of thanks, to Scott. It may very well have been his influence in Penelope's life that was the catalyst to get things moving forward for the two of them.

Nothing, but good times ahead.

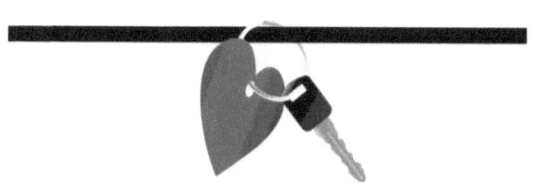

Epilogue

"Are they here yet?" Kyle ran into the kitchen, his face excited and hopeful.

Paul, sitting at the kitchen table, reached out to ruffle his nephew's dark hair. "Not yet, Sport."

Kyle nodded and turned to go back into the family room. "Soon?" He asked, pausing in mid-sprint.

"Definitely," Kris answered. She was pulling fresh muffins from her oven and placing them to cool on the countertop. "We'll call you kids the moment that they arrive."

Kyle flashed her a grin and resumed his sprint out of the kitchen.

"I don't envy you guys," Renee said, as she picked up Kris' carafe and poured them all fresh coffee. "That boy is going to be a charmer and a heartbreaker."

Kris laughed. "Just like his father. Don't worry, I'm fully aware and I'll whip him into shape, just like I did Grayson."

Paul laughed and shook his head.

"Oh!" Renee put the carafe down on the counter and cocked her head. The sound of the garage door signaled that Grayson had arrived and, more importantly, he wasn't alone.

Kris grinned with excitement and quickly called out to the kids. "Kyle! Round up the troops, they're here!"

A moment later the door opened, the kids swooped in, and general chaos ensued as Grayson led the way into the house.

"It's so good to see you!" Renee gushed, when she saw Penelope following Grayson, teetering between laughter and tears.

Paul squeezed her shoulder with one hand, while he reached out with the other to wrap an arm around his brother. Ben grinned and hugged him back.

Kris was patting at Penelope's face, as though she couldn't believe she was real, and Penelope pulled her forward into a tight hug.

"I missed you," Kris said, into Penelope's hair. "Three months is too long."

Penelope pulled back and grinned. "I know. Even though we kept in touch, it feels like a lifetime."

"Okay, okay," Grayson said, over the din. "Let's give them some air and let them into the house!"

Ben laughed as the kids untangled themselves from around their legs and disappeared into the family room. "I gotta say," he grinned, as they all made their way to the table and he pulled up a chair. "It really is great to be home."

"Oh," Renee gurgled, slapped her hands in front of her face and burst into tears. She was so happy that they were all back together, again, it was too much.

"Ren," Penelope said, reaching out to pat her shoulder. "Don't cry."

"It's okay," Renee insisted as she swiped at her eyes. "I'm just really happy that you guys are home, safe and sound, and -- Oh!"

"What?" Kris looked at Renee, alarmed.

Renee's eyes were wide and she pointed, with short jabbing motions, at Penelope's left hand. "Wedding ring!" She blurted, causing both Ben and Penelope to crack up.

"What!" Kris lunged and grabbed Penelope's hand. Sure enough, alongside her engagement ring, she was wearing a slim, gold band.

"Yes," Ben said, a satisfied smile on his face. "We did it. We got hitched in London."

"Hey!" Grayson said, while Kris gave both Ben and Penelope hugs. "Congratulations!"

Paul nodded his head, pleased beyond words. Finally, he thought. It was about time.

"I'm jealous," Kris stated as she sat down beside Grayson, at the kitchen table. "We should have done that."

"Oh, come on!" Grayson blurted and started laughing. "No way!"

Kris gave him an indignant look, which made him laugh harder.

"Admit it," he said. "You were all about the fairy tale wedding and there's no way you regret it, or wish you'd done it differently."

Kris shrugged, and Renee started to laugh along with her husband. "He's got you," she said. "And, you know it!"

Kris smirked and took a sip of her coffee. They were right, of course. She had loved every minute of planning, and then experiencing, her wedding. She would have hated taking off and missing it. She caught Grayson's eye and winked. He raised an eyebrow, he knew it, too.

"Do you have pictures?" Renee asked, eagerly.

"Absolutely," Penelope said. "In fact, if you want to see some, at least the wedding ones, I can grab the SD card from the camera and we can show you."

"Gray," Kris pulled on Grayson's shirt. "Get your laptop."

Grayson nodded and stood up.

"Auntie Penelope!" Kyle burst back into the kitchen, followed by his two younger brothers and his twin cousins. "You have to see!" He grabbed her arm and attempted to drag her away from the kitchen table.

"Okay, Okay," she laughed. "I'm coming!"

"I'll get the camera," Ben told her as the children led her out of the room.

"Tada!" They all threw their arms out with a flourish, when they entered the living room, and Penelope grinned widely at how cute they all were.

"Wow!" She exclaimed as she looked at the huge mess before her. She knew that, for them, it was a creation. A form of pillow art. That being said, she couldn't help but be amused by the sheer volume of stuff that they had used to create to their masterpiece.

"It's a welcome home tribute," Kyle told her. "We all worked on it."

"Tell me exactly what I'm seeing," she enthused, and then listened closely as the children all jockeyed for a chance to fully explain their contribution to the creation on the living room floor.

"Okay, then," she said, once they were done. "I'll leave you to do some more. How does that sound?"

Kyle smiled his nine year old grin. "I'm happy that you and Uncle Ben are home."

Penelope felt as though her heart would burst open and had to restrain herself from grabbing him into a bear hug. "Me, too," she told him and kissed his cheek, before making her way back into the kitchen.

"What's going on," she asked when she was greeted by five, goofy, grinning faces. "Have you started on the photos?"

Ben stood up and moved around the table to embrace her. "I told them," he whispered into her ear.

Penelope pulled back and started to laugh. "I knew that you'd be the first to crack!"

It was all that she was able to say, before her family began to clamor around them, all speaking words of congratulations.

"We get to be Aunties!" Renee enthused as she grabbed Kris' arm. "Together!"

Grayson and Paul laughed and then Grayson sparkled obnoxiously at Paul. "Us, too! We get to be Uncles, together!"

"Oh, quiet, you!" Kris said to her husband, and then, because it was funny, giggled.

"Time for celebration cake!" Renee managed to throw in, above the din of conversation. "Someone get the kids."

I'll do it," Ben offered and gave Penelope a quick kiss on the cheek as he moved past her toward the family room.

He stood in the doorway, paused and watched them play. They were fantastic. And, soon, he, too, would be someone's father. It both amazed him and terrified him. The best part, however, was that it was with Penelope. She gave his life ... Life.

"Everything okay?"

Ben turned to find his wife standing behind him, her face radiant. "Life," he said, and then slipped his arm around her waist. "I'm better than ever."

THE END

Turn the page for a Sneak
Peek at Kathleen Kole's
fabulous new novel,

Dollars to
Donuts.

Available, Summer 2011.

CHAPTER 1 - Friday

5:55 a.m.

"Auug!" April yelled as she hit the brakes on her metallic-blue mountain bike, sending her rocketing like a cannon ball over the handlebars.

"Oh-my-God!" She squealed, when she landed on her hands and knees with a squishy thud right in the middle of a copious mud puddle on her side lawn.

"Damn it!" April blurted, shocked. Things had happened too quickly. One moment she was leaving on her bike, the next there was a blur of fur and then, before she could say "What the?", she was off of her bike being assaulted by cold, oozing mud. Her brain was trying frantically to connect the dots and she was finding it a challenge to catch her breath.

A screen door creaked loud and long and April turned to see her neighbor, Carol, resplendent in a riotously flowered housecoat and beige, shaggy slippers, exiting her house.

"Oh, fudge," April exhaled. She was splattered from head to toe with dripping, mucky water and now, this?

"April!" Carol called out, shuffling down her front steps and across the lawn, her hot pink rollers jostling merrily in her brown hair.

"Hey, Carol," April gave a small, stiff wave and grimaced when mud oozed from her hand down her arm. Gross. She had to get up off of her knees.

"What on Earth?" Carol's eyes were wide and her mouth flapped open, then closed, like a fish inside a glass bowl.

"Seems I had a bit of a mishap," April replied, through a tight smile, willing herself to stay calm. In the few months that she'd lived in her new cul-de-sac, she'd had more than her share of neighbor encounters to inspire patience. She could just add this one to the list. If things kept up, she'd end up with the composure of a Monk.

"And then some," Carol added, as she watched April lean toward the grass and try to wipe her hands clean. It didn't work. Instead, she was left with small bits of green grass stuck to her palms.

"When I heard you scream," Carol continued, her face contorted in a grimace as she pressed a hand to her ample chest and shuddered. "I thought the worst, I'm sorry to say. Maybe a hate crime... I've been watching the news."

Oh, Jeez, not more talk of the news, April thought. She eased herself up out of the muck and imagined that she probably looked like some sort of movie creature, emerging from the ooze to terrorize the town. Judging by the way that Carol took a fast step backward, April guessed she wasn't far off.

"Do I have dirt on my face? It feels like it might be in my teeth."

"You're just filthy," Carol said, matter of fact, wrinkling her nose.

"You think?" April spat a piece of grit from her mouth and wiped her nose with the back of her hand. Carol took another small step backward.

"And, your bicycle," Carol glanced at April's bike laying inelegantly on the ground, pursed her lips and shook her head. "I remember when my girls were young, Edward and I were adamant that they take care of their belongings."

April blanched. Was Carol comparing her daughter's once-upon-a-time, childish negligence to what was in front of her? Unbelievable.

"We always told them that it only takes a moment," Carol blathered.

"Sometimes you cannot plan ahead, Carol," April cut her off, her words clipped as she wiped her dirty palms on her soiled grey hoodie. "For instance, I could never have predicted when I was innocently trying to leave my property, that your dog would be the reason I ended up in the mud at the crack of dawn."

"Peaches?" Carol's face lit up and she looked around expectantly.

"Over there," April pointed a grubby finger toward the flowerbeds in Carol's yard. The shaggy, blonde Cocker Spaniel was sprawled comfortably in the soft grass, watching the show.

"Has my Sweetums been playing with you?" Carol shook her head, making her rollers wobble, and giggled.

"Playing?" April echoed, flicking bits of grass from her sleeve to the ground. "Well, if you call dashing in front of a moving bike *playing*--"

"You may not know this," Carol confided, as she adjusted the sash on her flowered robe. "But, one of her favorite games is Chase."

"Yeah," April said, her voice laced with sarcasm as she shook each of her legs in an attempt to rid her navy blue sweatpants of muck. Nothing budged. "I picked up on that."

"It doesn't matter what it is," Carol added, tucking her hands into her pockets and smiling with great affection at her dog. "If she gets the notion in her head, look out."

April stared at her, at a loss for words. How, she wondered, does one respond to such blind devotion?

Carol peered at April's head. "Aren't you supposed to be wearing a helmet when you ride your bicycle?"

Shit, April thought. She had completely forgotten about her head. She snapped her hand in the air, then exhaled in shaky relief as her fingertips made contact with the makeshift turban she had fashioned out of an old, beige scarf. Thank goodness, it was still there. "Well," she said, ignoring Carol's question. "It's been interesting, but, I should be going--"

"Going?" Carol blinked and cast a skeptical look at April's soiled clothes.

April rolled her eyes. "It's just a little dirt. It will come right off." She shook her arm to prove her point. The mud didn't budge.

"And, besides," Carol cleared her throat. "Isn't it a bit, um, early for you?"

Good God. Did these people keep time cards or something?

"I mean," Carol blustered, patting at her pink hair rollers. "Not that I'd know when you usually go out..."

April sighed and bent down to get her bike. She knew that she couldn't win, better to quit while she was ahead. She wrapped her fingers firmly around the bike's handle bars and then, just as she was about to pull the bike upright, her carefully wrapped scarf decided it was time to defect from her head.

"Good gracious!" Carol clapped a hand across her mouth, her eyes wide and round like saucers.

"Oh, come on!" April blurted, when the scarf unraveled, slipped off and the summer breeze hit her exposed head. It was too much. Her hair, an embarrassing shade of florescent orange and a mess of awkward angles, made her look like a badly maligned Muppet.

"A-A-April!" Carol sputtered, like a can of used up whipped cream.

Fudge it, April thought. Good neighbor charade be damned. She had dressed in the most bland, least obvious clothes that she could find in her closet for one reason: to get out of her cul-de-sac without being observed by any of her prying-eyed-nosey-neighbors and get on with her day. Did it work? No. Apparently leaving like a normal person, undetected by the people on her street, was not an option.

"What? How?" Carol began.

"Spit it out, Carol!" April's voice was menacing with barely suppressed rage. She tightened her grip on her handle bars, snapped her head in Carol's direction and stared her in the face. She'd hit the wall. "What is it you're trying to say?"

Carol leaned back sharply. Apparently, circumstances made it unimportant that April was only 5'2", on a good day. Having a face that was streaked with mud, hair that appeared jolted by electricity and breathing like a half crazed dragon took precedent over anything else.

"W-w-well," Carol stammered and wrung her hands together. "What I meant to say is... Well, Dear, your *hair...*"

"Whow thare!"

Peaches, pretty much forgotten in the midst of the chaos, jumped to her feet at the sound of the booming voice and yapped a few times, ready for action.

"You have got to be kidding me," April groaned in disbelief.

It was Thomas, their Scottish neighbor, his brogue almost as thick as the knee high grass in his yard. He popped his head out from behind some ratty, tangled shrubs and April wondered just how long he'd been there, before deciding to make his entrance.

"Ay, yur quite the sight thaur, arn ye lass?"

April pushed her kick stand down, leaned her bike on it and rubbed at her temple as the first twinges of a headache threatened. "Friend of yours?" She asked Carol. Carol recoiled and April snickered. Apparently not.

Thomas ambled through his overgrown yard, ducking beneath the long, untamed branches of his oak trees as he moved toward them. He puffed on a cigarette that dangled from his lips, causing a thin trail of smoke to follow in his wake.

As April watched him approach, she found herself briefly envisioning the man as a toddler, a cigarette tucked in his mouth instead of a pacifier. It was a reasonable notion - she had never seen Thomas without his habit of choice in all the days she'd lived in the neighborhood.

"Goan thein," Thomas prompted, once he stood squarely in front of April. "Tell us, whot's this, retro meets bairnyard chic?"

April scowled at him, while he rocked back and forth on his heels, a glint of mirth shining in his eyes. She wanted so badly to tell him to flake off, but, she didn't. All in the name of neighborly preservation.

Instead, she eyeballed his outfit with barely disguised contempt. He was sporting a pair of red plaid pajama pants, a stained, green sweater and a pair of yellow-tinted workshop glasses pressed against his forehead. Combined with his head of unkept, salt and pepper hair and Van Dyke beard, the man looked like he was out on a day pass.

"I'm-sure-I-don't-know-what-you-are-talking-about." April punctuated each word with a flick of her hand to dispel the smoke that had begun to form in a cloud around her face. It wasn't just the smoke that was bothersome, it was his cigarette, too, that made her very nervous. That fiery tip, so close to her highly flammable hair... Yikes.

Thomas didn't so much as flinch and April felt defeat firmly shroud her shoulders. Clearly, he'd missed her point entirely and she was, quite frankly, exhausted. It was time to retreat and eat donuts. Besides, she mused, while gazing at her mud caked clothes and reflecting upon her catastrophic hair, facts were facts - she wasn't fit for the public eye. Time to say Uncle.

"Well, I guess that's it, then." April flicked the kick stand on her bike with the toe of her dirty sneaker and firmed her grip on the handle bars. Peaches stood up and wagged her tail, eager to see what April would do next.

"No, no, Sweetums," Carol cooed as April scowled at the dog. "You can't play with April any more, today."

April rolled her eyes and dragged her bike around the mud puddle. Play, indeed.

"Oh!" Carol blurted as April began to move away. "What about your scarf?"

"Don't need it, don't care," April called over her shoulder as she walked across her lawn toward her house.

Thomas looked up at the rapidly darkening sky. "Leuks like we might hae a bit 'o the lashing doan," he commented, the motion of his lips causing ash at the tip of his cigarette to scatter down across his green sweater.

What? April paused to looked back at her neighbors. Judging by the confused expression on Carol's face as she retightened the sash on her robe, it was clear that she had not understood Thomas' speculation that they might be in for rain.

April cast an appraising eye at her Scottish neighbor and wondered what his deal was. He had to be in his early sixties, definitely not new to the area and, yet, how was it that he was still speaking like a countryman who had just hit dry land? She decided to test him and called back, "Yup, should get inside before it starts, or at least get an umbrella."

Thomas snapped his head in her direction and April snickered under her breath at the surprise on his face. *Curious*, she thought, nodding to herself as she pushed her bike across the remainder of the yard and leaned it up against the side of her house. Clearly, he hadn't expected her to understand him.

"Might even want to grab a Mac," she couldn't help adding, just to stir it up. Thomas furrowed his brow, making his shop glasses look like a second pair of yellow eyes on his forehead, and April giggled.

Let him stew on that, she thought as she turned on her heel, sprinted across her lawn and up the steps to the solitude of her house. She slipped inside and slammed the front door so hard behind her that the white shutters on the windows rattled.

About the Author

Kathleen began storytelling in grade school and has many fond memories of passing summer afternoons, out on the swings in her backyard, creating tales that entertained her neighborhood friends.

Many years later, too many to talk about without seeming rude and nosey, Kathleen has channeled her imagination to the pages of her novels. She hopes that you enjoy her tales and encourages you to feel free to read her stories on the swing set in your own backyard.

Kathleen now spends time in her backyard with her beloved husband, adored son and silly dog. They let her tell them stories and always laugh in all of the correct places. She's lucky, and she knows it.

Please visit Kathleen's website to find out about her next novel, *Dollars to Donuts*.

Connect with Kathleen Online

Website: www.KathleenKole.com
Facebook: www.facebook.com/KathleenKoleAuthor
Twitter: www.twitter.com/KathleenKole